NORMAN LAZENBY

LITA'S LAMENT

Complete and Unabridged

LINFORD
Leicester

First published in Great Britain

First Linford Edition
published 2010

British Library CIP Data

Lazenby, Norman A. (Norman Austin)
    Lita's lament. - - (Linford mystery library)
    1. Private investigators- -California- -
Los Angeles- -Fiction. 2. Organized crime- -
California- -Los Angeles- -Fiction.
    3. Detective and mystery stories.
    4. Large type books.
    I. Title II. Series
    813.5'4–dc22

ISBN 978–1–84782–981–8

Published by
F. A. Thorpe (Publishing)
Anstey, Leicestershire

Set by Words & Graphics Ltd.
Anstey, Leicestershire
Printed and bound in Great Britain by
T. J. International Ltd., Padstow, Cornwall

This book is printed on acid-free paper

LITA'S LAMENT

Lita Rossini was a model; a would-be showgirl and a magnet for grief. When she visited the apartment of nightclub owner Abe Craster, hoping to advance her career, she was the unwitting catalyst for Craster to drop down dead! Fleeing the scene, she encountered private eye Jerry Randell, who was investigating Craster's criminal activities. The consequences of that meeting would not only bring more grief to Lita, but also to Jerry — and various members of Los Angeles' crooked underworld!

1

She was getting out of Abe Craster's apartment fast as hell, and because Abe had locked his door there was only one way she could think about — the fire escape. Lita Rossini got through the bedroom window and placed a high-heeled shoe on the metal platform. She looked back fearfully, although there was little chance that Abe Craster would leap at her.

The man was dead!

She hadn't killed him. He had died of a heart attack.

He had wanted to play games and she had produced the little .25 gun and stabbed him with the muzzle — just like that.

But it had been enough to scare hell out of him. He had been taken with a seizure. In fact, he had died under her horrified eyes.

So Lita Rossini was getting out of it.

She clutched her handbag containing her heater, and she went fearfully down the first few steel steps of the fire escape. It was dark, except for the flashing of a nearby neon sign across the alley. When the neon flashed into life to describe the virtues of Stolz's beer, there was an unearthly reddish glow that was enough for her to see her way down the escape.

Lita was a redhead, with the body of a model — which was in fact her occupation. And as Lita Rossini drew the men just like she was a magnet, she also drew grief.

Grief and Lita were seldom apart!

And this seemed to be another lousy setup — just the sort of thing that would happen to her! So Abe Craster had to go die on her instead of being nice and promising her that job in his nightspot. He shouldn't have tried it on with a girl half his age. She hadn't known he had a bad heart. It seemed like the man was rotten with drink and corruption. She had been a fool to go to his apartment. It was well known that Abe Craster was a crook in addition to his nightclub activities.

Lita went down the escape with a clatter of high heels on metal. Then she got to the end of the contraption. She saw a ten-foot drop. She would have to lower herself over the edge of the escape and trust that the drop was not too bad. It was dark in the alley. She cursed the setup, and she knew some choice words. She didn't like the dirt on her hands. But there was no going back. Not for any damn thing was she returning to that apartment and the grotesquely sprawling figure of Abe Craster.

She hung from the last step of the escape and then, with a momentary hesitation, let go.

She hoped to land on her feet.

But she didn't. Instead she felt strong arms grab her. She had fallen into a man's arms!

Lita Rossini immediately struggled, her first thought being that this man was a cop. It flashed on her — why should he be standing in the darkness near this fire escape? Then he spoke.

'Say, what gives? Why'd you come down the escape? Leads from Abe

3

Craster's apartment, doesn't it? Let me see you, baby!'

It was a mocking voice and Lita judged the man to be tall, strong. She saw a firm jaw and a handsome face as the nearby neon flooded red haze into the alley. He was wearing a snapbrim hat and she could not see much more.

'Let me go!' she snapped. 'Who the hell are you, anyway? Let me go!'

'I'm Jerry Randell. Now c'mon — what gives? Why leave Abe's apartment by the escape? Did the old slob get rough, huh?'

'Yeah, he got rough!' Lita said defiantly. 'Now will you let me go? It's no business of yours.'

'Well, now, sugar, that's not strictly true. Anything to do with Abe Craster is my business. Well, okay, so he got tough, wanted to play games, I guess. How come he didn't come after you? What did you do — hit him on the snozzle?'

'You talk too much, Mister Jerry Randell,' snapped Lita. 'Oh, damn you! Let go of my hands!'

She twisted lithely, and the next instant managed to dart away from him. But at the very outset she dropped her handbag. There was no chance to retrieve it. She was glad to be free of his grip, and she thrust into a lightning run.

Jerry Randell made the mistake of stopping to pick up her handbag. And Lita was surprisingly fast. She was only nineteen and late nights and drinking had not yet sapped her energy. She could move and she went on propelled by fear. She still had a mental picture of the hideously sprawled figure of Abe Craster. The scare was still with her.

She rushed out onto a brightly illuminated street and mingled with the crowds, now walking quickly. She went along the streets of Los Angeles.

She threw a backward glance and decided that the interfering Jerry Randell was not in pursuit or, if he was, she had lost him. That was fine.

Then she realised she had lost her handbag, too. She swore bitterly for that bit of leather had cost her plenty.

She had also lost her gun and a few dollars cash. It could have been worse; she had left most of her dough at home, in a little cash box. Not that she ever had much money; it seemed to melt as fast as she earned it. But then, she lived right up to the last buck and one of her troubles was that lately she had had to sell her auto to buy some new clothes. Clothes, to a model were important. And, too, she'd ambitions to sing in a nightspot. That was why she'd seen Abe Craster. Now she wished to hell she hadn't gone to his apartment. When he was found dead, would her name be remembered? Could be, because the Japanese valet who had shown her in had had her name.

The whole thing left a nasty taste in her mouth. On the impulse Lita Rossini walked into a drinking joint. She knew the neon-hung dive; had been in the red-plush place before. It was simply named: Joe's Place. It lay on the corner of Pico and Lincoln Boulevard.

She sat on a stool and got herself a martini and thought bitterly of the undignified way she had left Abe Craster's apartment.

A man near her thought she was showing plenty of nyloned leg on purpose to attract him. Defiantly, glancing at him, she slid her dress hemline down a bit and turned her head.

And then a man came up to her. She knew him — Tommy Berg, a guy with an 'in' to the entertainment world, few scruples and probably some crook side-lines like dope running.

He was a likeable type who wore flashy clothes and a grin. The reckless grin was always there. Tommy Berg liked women and found Lita attracted him like an irresistible magnet,

She glanced into his dark eyes and exclaimed: 'Gosh, Tommy Berg — just the guy I need. Lend me a buck, will you? I got to pay for this martini yet and the bartender is giving me suspicious looks although I've been here a lot.'

'You broke, baby?' Tommy grinned back.

'I lost all my dough — 'cept for some back home. I just lost my handbag.'

'Some plug-ugly snatch it?'

'Oh, no. I — I — just lost it, Tommy. Be a good guy and pay for my drink.'

'For you, sugar, anythin'. How about

you an' me going some place cosy after this drink, huh?'

'Your apartment?' she mocked. 'For the price of a martini? Forget it, Tommy!'

'Okay, okay!' Tommy Berg grinned easily, conscious that this reckless smile had worked wonders with a long list of women.

He paid the bartender and ordered another two drinks. He had a nicely stuffed billfold. It seemed right now Tommy Berg was in the potatoes. Sometimes he was not!

'We're not going to your apartment,' Lita emphasised. 'As a matter of fact, I think I'll go home.'

'Early, ain't it? Maybe you could invite a lonely guy?'

'No invitation,' said Lita firmly, and her green eyes glinted mockingly. 'Anyway, I'm out of eats back home.'

'Who said anything about eats?' he murmured.

Lita Rossini laughed in his face. 'Aw, take the line somewhere else, Tommy. You oversexed ginks are all the same. How's business?'

'Changin' the subject, huh? Okay. Business is fine — and I've a proposition for you. You get around, kid, and you must get to know people. You ever figure you could make some easy mazuma peddling dope?'

'Nothing doing!' said Lita coolly. 'I get around, sure, but I've also got ambitions to be somebody. You want to distribute dope, go ahead! I don't think I'd like the business, pal.'

He gestured placatingly. 'Okay, okay, don't raise your voice — you never know who is on the anti-narcotic squad these days. Just figured you might like to pick up some dough, that's all.'

'I could do with some money,' said Lita bitterly. 'Things aren't too good for me. Oh, I've got my salary as a model, but I've been spending too much. I had to sell my auto. I even went to see Abe Craster — ' She broke off, realising she had not wanted to say that much.

'You been to see Abe Craster?' he jerked. 'Well, he is in the dope racket in addition to that ritzy nightspot he runs. Not that me an' Abe are pals. He's tried to hoof me out of the dope business — wants all the contacts. He's big, I admit. Got dough to hire guys an' I haven't. So you went to see the fat slob? Why, baby?'

'Forget it!' she suddenly hissed. 'I — I — just figured he might give me a job singing in his club — that's all — aw, hell, I'm going home. Be seeing you. Tommy!'

'Now, look — ' he began, but she had slipped from the red-topped stool and was swiftly making towards the exit.

Lita Rossini hurried out into the neon-hazed night and once more walked quickly along the sidewalks. She was definitely going home! She would get home, lock her door and take a scented bath and then go to bed. A girl ought to have beauty sleep — she had read about that in magazines, and she wanted to remain beautiful.

Her apartment was not far away and she could walk the distance. She'd have to, in any case, because she had no money for a cab and taxi-drivers sometimes got tough with passengers who asked them to wait until they went indoors for the fare!

Lita Rossini's apartment was on the fourth floor of a big block on Culver Boulevard. It was a big old building and not too classy. Even so the rent was high. Only a mile away was the sea at Santa Monica Bay. And Wiltshire Boulevard, which ran not far away, led to the heart of the swank Beverly Hills. She was only two miles from Hollywood and a gang of folks who lived the big-time. But she was just one of a thousand pretty girls.

Swiftly tapping high heels brought her to the apartment house. She went up the stairs — it was that kind of block; there wasn't an elevator.

Only at her door did she realise she had lost her key. It was in her handbag! Angrily she put a hand on the doorknob and shook it.

To her surprise the door opened!

She knew she had locked it when she had set out. Slowly she walked into the apartment. She hadn't long to wait for her second shock.

A man sat in her best easy chair! He was, she realised instantly, Jerry Randell. This was the character who had grabbed her at the bottom of Abe Craster's fire escape. So he had found her handbag! That was how he had gotten her address and her key. Well, she'd tell him where to get off! She faced him, a lithe girl whose lovely body trembled with fury under the smart and fashionable clothes. She saw amused grey eyes, that strong jaw and firm lips — now twisted in a smile. He had his hat on his knees, and she saw crisp, wavy black hair. Yeah, he was a handsome guy, no mistake. Seemingly he had plenty of nerve, too!

She lashed out: 'How dare you come here? If you've got my handbag, leave it and scram! So you opened the apartment! Of all the goddam nerve — '

He got out of the chair like a coiled spring; came to her. She swung a furious fist, but he stopped it; held her hands. 'Cool down, sister. Yeah, I've brought back your handbag — complete with gun, dough, powder, lipstick and a visiting card. The card says you're Lita Rossini, model. Now, sister, I know that Abe is dead.'

That stopped her fighting! She stared

into his grey eyes and thought she saw a decent guy. But who was he?

'Let's sit down,' he said quietly.

They sat down in chairs opposite to each other. He did not speak. He held out a gold cigarette case and they lit up. All that took time. Lita calmed considerably before he began talking again. 'Yeah, I went around to Abe Craster's apartment just after you ran away from me. The Japanese servant and me found the guy dead. A doctor lives in that apartment block, and we got him on the job. Then the doc informed the police.'

'The police!' Lita gasped. 'But they can't blame me! He — he — just died! He tried to paw me — I stuck my gun in his ribs and — and — he just died! Oh, it scared me!'

Jerry Randell nodded. 'The doctor said he died of natural causes. The cops had to be told because the butler was yammering about a girl who had been in the apartment with Abe. I gave the cops all I knew, but didn't tell 'em about finding your handbag.'

'You didn't tell them about me?'

'No. I figured you'd report to the cops yourself after you'd had time to think. You'll be okay. You've done nothing wrong. Better to report. I know Lieutenant Dick Strang — he's a right guy.'

'You know him? Who are you, anyway?'

He smiled. 'I'm Jerry Randell, private detective.'

Lita expelled breath in relief. 'I — I — thought you might be some louse. A private eye! So you were snooping around Abe Craster's place. Why?'

He leaned forward. 'That fat slob was in the dope racket. His night club didn't really pay but it was a good place for dope runners and customers to meet. Sure, there was a normal business as a front, with good cooking and entertainment. But it wouldn't have paid except for the profits from the dope trade. Now Abe Craster had a map in his safe showing the location of a huge consignment of cocaine. This consignment was hidden somewhere and the value is enormous. There is enough dope cached away to supply every hophead in Los Angeles for about a year. That's big! The stuff came up from Mexico by truck — secretly, of course, because the anti-narcotic squad were on the look-out for it. The rumour had gotten around. Somehow the cleverest secrets escape into the underworld. But the cops couldn't pin anything on Abe Craster and they didn't grab the truck carrying the dope in spite of great efforts. The cocaine was cached somewhere. And Abe Craster was the only one with the location. The truck-driver is dead. He was found last night with a slug in the back of his head — in a dark alley. Abe Craster saw to that. Abe made a map and he kept it in his safe.'

'But, gosh, how do you know all this?' gasped Lita.

Jerry Randell let smoke trickle from firm lips. 'That story is a build-up from many sources of information. For instance, it's no longer a secret about the existence of the consignment of drugs. Every lousy crook in L.A. knows about it. It was a rumour that just crept out — I admit I don't know how. The truck-driver talked about Abe having a map of the location in his safe. That was just a slip of a few words in a barroom! And Abe promptly hired a gunny to bump the guy off!'

Lita shivered. 'And to think I went to that slob's apartment! But why are you telling me all this?'

Jerry Randell flicked his cigarette. 'Because while I was in Abe's apartment I was lucky enough to get the safe open while the doc and Japanese butler were phoning the cops. I have some nifty keys, and Abe's safe was as old as the hills. I opened it in seconds, but I didn't find any map. Plenty of bills on account of the nightspot, a wad of dough, some letters that were of no account — but nothing resembling a map.'

'Did you look carefully?'

'I did, baby. I shot a glance at every item. No damned map. And now to the reason why I'm telling you all this: I want to know if Abe Craster opened his safe while you were in the apartment. Did he open his safe? Did he promise you any money? He didn't give you any because there wasn't much in your handbag. But maybe he opened his safe and took something out? Did he put anything in his pockets?'

'Only the key of the door,' rapped Lita. 'No, he did not open his safe. And he did not give me any dough, Mister Jerry Randell. I was there simply to coax a job out of the slob. He got the wrong idea of how far I figured to go!'

'So he did not open the safe and transfer anything — perhaps an envelope — to his pocket!' muttered Jerry.

'Wouldn't you have found the envelope or map if he'd put it in his pocket?' asked Lita. 'Didn't the police search the — the body?'

'Yeah,' said Jerry Randell grimly, 'they did, naturally. And, confidentially, so did I after looking in the safe. No dice! But, I thought if maybe he'd transferred the map to his pockets, somebody might have got hold of it.'

'You mean me?' flared Lita.

'No. Not you. You knew nothing about this.'

'Well, who?'

'The Japanese butler-valet,' snapped Jerry. 'He could have found Abe dead before I called. He'd have a few minutes — and minutes were all he needed. He'd know the rumours about the terrific value of the dope that's cached.'

'Well, I don't know if Abe had the map in his pocket,' said Lita, 'but I do know he didn't open the safe in my presence. Nope, he just started the old funny stuff routine — before he snuffed it. Now one more question, Mister Private Richard: why are you investigating all this? You working for the cops, huh?'

Jerry Randell rose to his full six feet and grabbed his hat. 'I'm hired to investigate. A wealthy guy has a daughter who is ruined by taking dope. She's being nursed back to health, at her home, privately, and it's one helluva job. This girl got her dope from Abe Craster. This girl's father hates the dope trade and everything it stands for. He's got enough wealth to hire me to find that cache of cocaine and destroy it.'

'Why not let the cops do it?' questioned Lita.

'This wealthy guy wants fast results. He'll laugh like hell when he learns that Abe Craster is dead. But that still doesn't locate the dope.'

'If no one but Abe knew where to find the dope,' said Lita, 'why worry?'

'That map is somewhere,' said Jerry grimly. 'And it's worth a small fortune to some louses.'

Lita threw her cigarette stub away, into the dead fire. 'Thanks for bringing my bag and the information. I guess I'll report to the cops. Will you come with me? I'd like to get it over with. Anyway, I'm not responsible for that slob's bum heart!'

'I'll take you,' agreed Jerry. 'Then I want to quiz that Japanese servant. I should have grabbed him before I came here. I got a lousy feeling that smooth little rat has the map.'

They went down to the street. Jerry had an auto parked around a corner. But the dark corner also held two thugs who rammed guns into Jerry and Lita!

2

The surprise was complete. Jerry Randell, like most private Richards, held a licence to carry a heater and he wore it in the usual shoulder holster. But to attempt to withdraw it meant calling the bluff of the two thugs. Maybe they would shoot to kill; maybe they would not.

Jerry Randell thought maybe there were other ways out of this little trap. And he wanted to know what it was all about!

So he froze. Lita stood stock still — but it was because she was scared!

'What's this, fellers?' snapped Jerry. 'If you're muggers, you've got a rod on a private dick! You won't get more'n a few bucks outa me and I'll remember ya!'

'Shuddup!' snarled one man. He moved a little and Jerry saw a blue chin, rat-trap mouth and big bulbous nose. He didn't know the guy, but then he didn't know every damned crook in Los Angeles.

The other man who was holding the heater on Lita Rossini was a slight, wiry gink in a wine-red suit. Another stranger!

'Look,' said the first man, 'don't let's have grief. Let's do this businesslike. We got the drop on ya an' if we trigger it'll be hellish messy. Got it? Now, sister, where's that damn map ya took from Abe Craster's place?'

'Jeeze!' yelped Jerry Randell. 'Somebody else onto it!'

'Shaddup, you!' snarled the blue-chin rat-mouth. 'We know you — Jerry Randell, the shamus! We know Abe Craster is dead, too. We know a helluva lot!'

'Seems like it,' agreed Jerry. 'Supposin' we have a little confab, huh?'

'The map!' snarled the man. 'This ain't no place for confabs. Who's got the map — you or the dame? Hand over.'

'Get it straight, buster,' jeered Jerry, 'neither Lita Rossini nor I have the map. How'd you know where to find her, anyway?'

'We've had a stooge planted in that apartment of Abe Craster's, watching the slob, an' he saw this dame arrive. This guy recognised this dame — knew she was pally with a guy called Tommy Berg. We've just been talkin' to Berg in Joe's Place. It was only minutes to figure out the whole play. We got over here. We heard you two talkin' inside the apartment an' we figured to wait until you'd gone, bud. Then we'd get the dame — and the map. But seems you two figure to go some place.'

'Thanks for the yap, feller,' sneered Jerry Randell, 'Yeah, we figured to go see Lieutenant Strang at headquarters. Maybe you'd like to come along, too?'

'The map! Who has it? C'mon, give!'

'You get hellish monotonous, buster! We ain't got the map so what do you figure to do about it. So far as I know, the map is in Abe Craster's safe,' Jerry bluffed.

'Like hell it is! After the cops took the body away in the ambulance, me and Rick got onto that Japanese butler. We made him find the key to the safe. When we opened up, there sure wasn't a map inside. So we figured it out: this dame got the map. She got into the safe while Abe was lyin' dead. Nobody else could have done it!'

'You've jumped to some dandy conclusions,' agreed Jerry Randell. 'But you're onto the wrong lead, fellers! The man you want is the Japanese guy.'

'Don't give us that!' The gun pressed grimly into Jerry's side. 'We figure the dame got the map. Don't try pull that Japanese angle over on us. Looks like you're tryin' to horn in on that cache of dope.'

'When I get it,' said Jerry frankly, 'I'll have it burnt!'

'Yeah? You're crazy! Why, that stuff must be worth a lotta dough.'

'And a lot of grief for some people. Who are you two characters, anyway?'

'I'm Cal Owen,' growled blue-chin. 'An' this is Rick Egler — so what! Brother, you got just three seconds to live. Your bluff sure proves to me the dame has that goddamn map. You — '

Whether the man had wanted to confab or not, he was sure doing a lot of talking and it was his downfall.

His yap gave Jerry Randell just that odd second in which to try some tricky play. Actually, there wasn't much choice for Jerry; he recognised in a flash that these two thugs would kill if the stalling process went on any longer. They believed, rightly or wrongly, that Lita Rossini had the map.

Jerry Randell slammed his hands down at the gun pressing into his ribs. His move was like a jag of lightning, as fast and as violent. It had to be. He slammed hands down at the gun and deflected it in a smashing second, before Cal Owen could trigger. The gun did not explode. The man was pushed back simultaneously with the first movement, and he crashed against Rick Egler.

Jerry Randell jumped in front of Lita, pushing her back a bit. He yelled: 'Get into the auto and beat it!'

She obeyed, whether it was from fear or what she did not know. But she left the way clear for Jerry Randell, anyway.

He had Cal Owen tight against him to avoid giving the thug the chance to raise his gun. Then Jerry slammed the man hard back against his pal, Rick Egler, again. The two men were a confused huddle for some seconds. Jerry Randell, tough as hell and without scruples when dealing with louses, charged in with right and left fists swinging. He got his blows in terribly fast and they shuddered on the pans of Rick Egler and Cal Owen.

His triumph had no chance of lasting, Jerry knew that. He knew the thugs would back off, get some breath and either charge in or shoot him in the guts.

So he leaped back after the initial advantage had slammed the men into confusion. He leaped for his auto. He was helped by the fact that the door was swinging open. Lita Rossini was displaying sense besides a length of nyloned leg! As Jerry Randell flung into the car the girl released the clutch and the auto jumped away like a kangaroo! The car door shut itself under the momentum. It was some driving but it got them away damned fast!

Lita shot around the first corner and then snicked up to top gear. Gasping a bit, she stared through the windshield.

'I'm not at all sure how to drive this

auto,' she gulped. 'It's a bit different to the one I had!'

'Just keep it off the sidewalk,' said Jerry coolly. 'In fact, you can stop it an' I'll take over. We've lost off those birds.'

She did stop the car and was glad to relax while the private Richard tooled steadily down Culver Boulevard.

'Those birds got me mixed up,' he confessed. 'They think you took that lousy map.'

'That's crazy. I didn't know the first thing about it until you told me!'

'I believe that. Hell, I had it figured out that the Japanese servant was in this but now I'm not so sure. Aw, let's go see that smooth little gink before I take you along to Lieutenant Strang.'

'I don't want to go near that apartment again!' exclaimed Lita.

'Now take it easy. It won't take more than a minute for me to ring somethin' outa that butler.'

Some minutes of quick driving brought the auto outside the swank apartment block. Lita Rossini thrust her hands deep into her coat pockets and walked with her head held defiantly as she entered the lobby of the building. It seemed like a million years ago she had gone this same way; actually it couldn't have been more than an hour. Gee, what an hour! A guy had died, and she was pitched into a strange hell-around!

Going up in the elevator with Jerry Randell made it different to the last time. She glanced sideways at him; thought he was a nice chunk of beefcake. What did he do for love? Maybe he was married! All the best men were hitched! So this time she wasn't going to see an old slob to ask favours. Craster was dead. Somehow it seemed unreal, like a series of movie scenes on a dazed mind.

Jerry Randell pressed the bell of Abe Craster's apartment. He wasn't surprised when a uniformed cop answered the ring.

'You guarding the joint?' Jerry showed his licence automatically, although the cops knew him. 'I'd like to see the Japanese butler!'

'Walk in, shamus,' growled the cop, 'and try the Persian carpet. Lieutenant Strang sent me along after they took the body away — he figured the dope angle made this important, although I don't see what good it is havin' me stuck here. I think that story about a map is screwball. There ain't no map. Who says there was a map, anyway? Maybe it's all rumours.'

'Now look, Philo Vance,' began Jerry, 'there's a map. The truck driver who said there was a map was killed, remember? That lends substance to the theory.'

'Just a theory,' grumbled the cop. 'Who is this dame?'

'She is the girl who was with Abe when he died. The one the butler yammered about.'

The cop was surprised. 'Gee, you sure located her fast!'

Jerry Randell smiled. He thought there was no point in telling this cop about the handbag angle. He'd tell that to Lieutenant Strang. Maybe that policeman wouldn't like to know that Jerry had hung out on him, but he'd cool off.

There was a tenant in the block who was the spy planted by Cal Owen and Rick Egler. Of course, the police hadn't known about this guy. His identity, in fact, was still a secret. It wouldn't matter now. But the cops had never got around to asking this guy about the girl who had last been seen with Abe Craster. He, of course, had known Lita. Well, it was pointless now that Abe was so dead!

With the uniformed cop, Jerry Randell and the girl went through the big apartment to the little room adjoining the kitchen. This was the Japanese servant's quarters.

But there was no sign of him.

A ten-minute search of the apartment revealed the fact that the Japanese had gotten away by a rear exit to the block. He had emptied his clothes out of a chest of drawers — the drawers lay half-open.

'Beat it,' concluded Jerry. 'So?'

'So the butler has the map,' supplied Lita. 'He's your bad man!'

'Not that little runt,' said the cop, shaking his head. 'Lieutenant Strang figures the map was never in the safe, but hidden somewhere else.'

'Hell, don't complicate the thing,' grunted Jerry Randell. 'I think the butler could have got the map before I came up and asked to see Abe Craster.'

The cop yawned and said: 'So what?'

'What made you call on Abe Craster, anyway?' asked Lita curiously.

'I figured to scare him into making a move with that dope. That's all. A silly trick. It probably wouldn't have got me anywhere. So the butler an' me found Abe so dead. One thing just leads to another!'

'Let's get along to the cop station,' sighed Lita. 'This set-up is getting me down. Let's clear somethin' at least. If I give my story to Lieutenant Strang, it'll clear me out of this mess, anyway. And that's all I want. You can go chase around after the cache of dope, Mister Jerry Randell.'

At the Police Headquarters they found the lieutenant studying a dossier. He nodded as Jerry Randell and the girl were shown into the plain little office.

'This is Lita Rossini,' said Jerry, 'and she is the girl who was with Abe Craster when he died.'

Lieutenant Strang, a thick-set man of about forty, nodded but didn't look surprised. He'd stopped being surprised after his first twelve months with the cops.

All he said was: 'Neat work, locating her, Randell.' But after he had Lita's story down on paper and she had signed the statement, he growled: 'So you withheld information, Mr. Randell! You could have told me about finding this girl at the bottom of the fire-escape and her handbag!'

'Yeah, well, look, Dick, I — I — figured the girl was scared and she ought to have a break.'

'Okay.' The other smiled thinly. 'If we want an inquest, you'll give evidence, Miss Rossini. It'll only be a formality and won't take more than minutes. You two can go — and tell that rich client of yours to forget about Abe Craster's cache of dope!'

On that note, Lita and Jerry left the Police Headquarters. The girl was glad to go. 'You can take me home, Jerry,' she smiled. 'Then I'm having that scented bath and so to bed — with the damned door locked.'

'You really need someone to sleep on the landing,' said Jerry.

'Say, listen, you're working for this Roedeck guy, not me!'

'Yeah, but you're involved, Lita. How about Cal Owen and Rick Egler? Those two thugs think you might have the key to a small fortune. I'll make inquiries about those two crooks — might learn something.'

She smiled bewitchingly. 'Take me home, feller. Are all private dicks like you?'

'Aw, I'm just a guy.' They got into the car and he drove once again through neon-lit concrete chasms, The sidewalks were full of folks and other autos rolled down the streets on pleasure bent. It was not late at night and the inhabitants of El Pueblo du Nuestra Senora, la Reina de los Angeles (commonly known as L.A.) were moving around the haunts. There were plenty of people sitting at home by the side of TV sets, but you wouldn't think so, judging by the crowds on the main streets.

Reaching her apartment on Culver Boulevard, Lita wondered whether this Jerry Randell wanted a goodnight kiss!

3

He did. They talked at the door of the lobby of the apartment building, and then she asked him to have a drink. Inside her place, he had the drink, then set the glass down abruptly and pulled her into his embrace.

Lita reflected that he had helped her a lot, and responded by putting her arms round his neck.

After an interval she gently disengaged, and seated herself on a settee. As he sat next to her, she gave him a sideways glance. 'Where is this situation going? About the dope and everything, I mean?'

'This is how I see it,' Jerry said. 'Cal Owen and Rick Egler have a yen for this cache of dope an' they might return to this place for the ungodly purpose of knocking the map out of you. Now I figure the Japanese has the map.'

'Has this Japanese a damn name?' inquired Lita.

'Yeah. Sam Stong. That's his name.'

'So he's beat it, probably with the map,' commented Lita. 'How'd you expect to find him in this big city?'

'That's one helluva problem,' agreed Jerry grimly.

On the settee Lita stretched voluptuously. 'Well, I'm determined to have that scented bath, shamus. I've still got dirt on my hands from that so-and-so fire-escape.'

'I'll stick around,' said Jerry.

She widened her eyes. 'Now, look — '

'I mean I'll stay the night — in the living room if you want it, baby. Could be that Cal Owen and Rick Egler will make another call.'

'Put that way,' murmured Lita. 'I'll be glad if you stay the night. But let me tell you something, Mister Shamus, I ain't got time for this kind of game — I'm a model and I need to go to work.'

Jerry Randell stayed the night. After ninety minutes, of tossing and turning on the settee he eventually slept.

In the morning a ferocious alarm clock nearly burst his eardrums. He heard Lita

34

Rossini muttering something about work and getting out of the bed. She went to the bathroom, and after a not so brief toilet entered the living room, still wearing her filmy pyjamas. Jerry Randell, from the viewpoint of the couch, thought she looked fresh, delectable and fragrant. No wonder she was a model!

He went to the bathroom; later dressed and joined Lita as she prepared a breakfast. They ate in silence, smoked; she glanced continuously at her watch. She looked terribly attractive in a simple yellow dress that complicated the emotions. Lita wore a ton of lipstick on a pouting mouth. The morning sun made her green eyes cat-like. She looked at Jerry occasionally, contemplatively, calmly. She seemed to find something comforting in his cool grey eyes and strong jaw.

'I've a job to go to,' announced Lita.

'Oke. Those two thugs we tangled with seem to have flown. I got work to do, too. I wanna find Sam Stong.'

But before they got out of the apartment, the mailman called. They heard him grunting with exertion on the landing outside the apartment door; they heard the savage thump on the door and then the manilla envelope was slid under the door.

Jerry Randell smoked while Lita slit the envelope.

She spent a few slow seconds staring and then when she shot a glance at Jerry, he knew something was wrong.

'It's a letter!' she gasped.

'Yeah, I guess it is.'

She gulped. 'But it's from Abe Craster!'

'What?'

'And there's an envelope inside the first envelope which he wants me to mail back to him!'

Jerry Randell roared: 'What? Lemme see that envelope!'

She handed the whole lot to him, and the smile had left her crimson lips and she looked bewildered, frightened.

He held the letter and read:

'Dear Lita,
    You may be surprised to get this but I know you will help me. I, in turn, can be very helpful to the right sort of girl.

So don't fail me and you will find me a guy who is ready to give a big hand to the ambitious girl. I want you to mail the enclosed envelope. That's all. You will see that it is stamped and addressed to myself at a vacation cabin I own, just out of town near Tujunga Lake. It's a little business trick, as you might guess. Hold the envelope a few hours and mail at four-thirty on the day you get it, Don't fail me — but I know you won't, Lita,

Remember, I'm your pal and can do a lot for a swell girl like you.

Abe Craster.'

Jerry Randell looked up at Lita Rossini and they were both pretty astonished. With Jerry it didn't last much more than a few seconds, and during that time his brain was racing over the implications. Then, swiftly and grimly, he slit the other envelope. He thought it wasn't much use mailing it to Abe Craster at Tujunga Lake because unhappily the guy wouldn't be there to receive it! Abe had been pretty smart but he had not calculated rightly about his bum heart!

As he had expected, there was a cute little map inside the envelope and nothing else. The map was carefully drawn in red ink on a sheet of good white paper and had been carefully folded.

'This is it — the map!' Jerry gave a curt laugh. 'This is the key to the cache of dope which is worth a helluva lot of dough. This is what Cal Owen and Rick Egler want. And I figured the Japanese servant had it! Hell, I'm slippin'! Sam Stong must have beat it because he was scared. That's all.'

'Why should Abe Craster pick on me for this cute move?' snapped Lita.

'We'll never know his real intentions, but it looks like he was about to start a move to distribute some of that dope. He wanted to get away from his own apartment and his nightspot and he wanted the map at the cabin at Tujunga Lake. What better than an ordinary letter in the mail? He didn't want the letter to arrive at the cabin before he did and apparently he didn't want the map in his apartment any longer. So he picked on you, figuring you'd play ball without curiosity because you wanted favours from him.'

'Aw, gee!' Lita made a helpless gesture. 'Why didn't he want the map at his apartment?'

'Well, I'm just making guesses at his intentions, but maybe he realized too many other guys were interested in the cached dope and that he might have callers he couldn't cope with.'

'He could have mailed the letter to Tujunga Lake himself.'

'I've told you, Lita, he wouldn't want it lying around. If you mailed that letter at four-thirty today, it would be delivered tomorrow morning. Maybe Abe Craster figured to be at his cabin to receive it. He didn't expect to die, remember. He was using you as a stooge. Maybe he anticipated trouble at his apartment — some ginks who had an interest in that dope.'

'If he'd kept his hands off me, he'd have been alive!' snapped Lita.

'Maybe. He made a bad guess there.'

Lita flicked a finger at the map. 'Well,

you got it, shamus. You're the little boy who has the prize. Gee, what a crazy play! What are you gonna do with the map?'

'Locate the dope and burn it!' Jerry Randell walked across the room to the table and sat studying the drawing.

'Why don't you hand the map to the cops?' asked Lita. 'It's their job, isn't it?'

'I'm hired, remember, by Mr. Roedeck, who hates dope and the ginks who peddle it.'

'The map was sent to me!' snapped Lita.

'Yeah? So what? I got it now.'

'Oh, okay, go ahead and earn yourself some bucks! I suppose a private dick has to live.'

'You bet they have, an' I got a personal interest in this job now, Lita. I can burn that dope, make Roedeck happy, and then give the facts to Lieutenant Dick Strang. Now, look, this drawing indicates that the cache is near Tujunga Lake an' that cabin!' Looking at him, Lita Rossini thought the gleam in his grey eyes was almost boyish.

'I've never asked you,' she said. 'You married?'

'No!' he snapped. 'What the hell's that got to do with this map?'

'Nothin'! I was just thinking!'

'Sure, sure. Well, I got to be movin'.' He got up again; glanced at her. 'You still going to that modelling job?'

'Look, feller, I got to eat. I told you last night I wanted none of this hell-around.'

He nodded. 'Okay. I'll drop you off where you work. You ready? I wanna move. I'm really onto this job now!' And he tapped his gun under his armpit automatically.

She unlocked the apartment door. She stood beside him and he grinned at her. She had got into her street clothes and she wore a crazy hat and lace gloves up to her elbows. She hugged her handbag and he wondered if she still had the .25. He figured she would have.

'I'd kiss you,' he said. 'I got plenty of steam for you, but that lipstick would paint me like a Shawnee.'

'I'll take it as done,' said Lita. 'Okay, let's go — and if you're seen by the other

41

tenants this is where my rep is shot in the rear!'

His auto was in a nearby alley. He got it around to the street and Lita climbed in beside him.

As they tooled with the rest of the morning traffic down Culver Boulevard, she said, 'I work at Erlichs on Pico, 629.'

'What do you do — take off your damn clothes?' he growled.

'Yeah, sometimes. It's an art studio. But sometimes art is better with clothes.'

He stopped the auto at the address. It was a big white modern office block. Tall leaning palms sprouted up from a corner waste block. Lita Rossini got out of the auto.

'I don't even know where you live,' she said.

'I got an office on Slausen Street, and I sleep in a room above it. I get by, though being a private richard is a queer business. My number is 108 Slausen,'

'Thanks. I'll get your phone number from the book.'

She crossed the sidewalk and entered the lobby like a million-dollar heiress instead of a hard-up model. But she was jerked out of her classy stride by an arm that grabbed her. She jerked her head to see Tommy Berg's unsmiling face.

'You! What's this?'

'I wanna talk to you, baby. About Abe Craster.' He dropped the words huskily. 'All the junkies, hopheads and mainliners know about it now. You told me last night you'd been to see him. Now he's dead. There's rumours goin' around, baby. Gee, I wish I'd known last night you'd left the gink for dead. What d'ya know about the dope map, baby?'

Lita gasped and tried to free her arm. But his fingers were biting into her flesh.

'C'mon, give!'

'Tommy, you're crazy — I don't know anything about it!'

'Cal Owen and Rick Egler asked me about ya last night — wanted your address. I had to hand out. I didn't know then Abe Craster was dead. Now I get the picture. I saw ya drive up with that shamus guy — Randell, ain't it? Jerry Randell, the dick over on Slausen. Quite a guy. I got news from the grapevine about him, too. He's after that cached dope — but for different reasons.'

'You seem to know a lot!' she gasped.

Tommy Berg's reckless grin appeared again. 'Yeah — just bits here an' there. Maybe you can tell me somethin' more, Lita. What happened to the map?'

'I — I — don't know anything about it!'

'You said that the wrong way, chicken!' His dark eyes were suddenly cruel, 'C'mon, spill what you know. You do know somethin'. Did Cal Owen and Rick Egler call on ya last night?'

'Yes — no!'

'Make up ya mind, baby. I figure they did. They were hot pants for your address. Now they're pretty smart fellers. If they wanted to see you, it musta been important. Sure, they musta figured you knew somethin' about that goddamned map.'

His other hand came round and held her. At that moment the lobby was deserted, and Lita was suddenly scared. Tommy Berg was different; she realized the easy-going, reckless grin was mostly a front for a ruthless man.

'Let me go!' she panted.

'Not yet, chicken. You know somethin'. What is it?'

'I tell you I was simply mixed up with Abe Craster's death last night!' she said shrilly. 'You got the wrong ideas, you big lug!'

'I bank on hunches,' he gritted. 'And you know somethin' about that lousy map. That's worth dough, baby. C'mon — give out. Maybe I could pay you if ya help me.'

'Let go of me!' screamed Lita angrily.

'Don't be a flamin' fool!' he snarled, and he dragged her five yards across the lobby to a door set in a corner.

He was a smart guy, and knew the layout of the lobby seemingly. For the door gave access to a closet in which were arrayed the fuse-boxes and electric meters for the whole office block. It was a soundproof little room without windows. Tommy Berg shoved Lita into the hole and the door closed after them springily. Her despairing, frightened cry was cut off abruptly.

'Now don't think of bein' rescued!' he snarled, and his hands held her wrists to breaking point. She struggled and only increased the scared pumping of her heart and her heavy breathing. He played her in grim silence for nearly a minute, just proving his superiority. An electric light glowed eerily in the otherwise dim cubbyhole.

'Now talk!' he snapped.

'Not damned likely!' she screeched.

'You know somethin'. What is it? You don't want me to hurt ya, do ya?'

'You go to hell, Tommy Berg! I tell you I don't — '

'Don't give me that again!' he raged, 'I'm sick of it! What is Randell up to? What's his ideas? What did the cops say about Abe's death?'

But she only struggled, her lithe body jerking, her hands tugging futilely inside his grip. Her legs kicked out at intervals. She caught him on the ankle and he cursed. He moved his grip; held her with one hand and then brought his other hand across her face.

The pain of it brought tears to her eyes.

He slapped her again, wickedly, deliberately.

'I'm gonna muss ya up if ya don't talk,' he grated. He strengthened his grip on her arm and twisted sadistically. It was a lousy trick and Lita's green eyes bulged with horror and agony. He turned his hand like it was some instrument of torture. A hissing cry of pain escaped the girl's lips. She writhed, tried to yell but the sound would not come. She was past that. The pain and terror of being tortured had choked her throat.

Tommy Berg watched her viciously, his grin still incredibly there. But it was a brute grin. His hand gave Lita Rossini hell for some moments, almost tearing her flesh. The agony and fear sent her brain into a senseless haze, and she only surged out of it when he relaxed the cruel grip.

'Talk!' he gritted. 'Or there'll be worse!'

'You louse!' she managed to scream, 'I'll get Jerry Randell to kill you for this!'

'Yeah? So ya're thick, huh? C'mon — I want more.'

His bunched fist made a lightning dart at her face — and stopped only an eighth of an inch from her eyes. She had flinched back. She stared fearfully, wondering.

'Next time I hit your pan!' he hissed. 'Any more goddamn stallin' from you an' I'll scrape half the skin off ya face! You wouldn't like that — a model! What's it to be before I really get tough? C'mon, ya crazy bitch! Why the hell be so stubborn?'

His hand moved again and it was too much for Lita Rossini. She gave a tiny scream and flattened against the wall and let loose a torrent of words. She just couldn't help it.

'No! No! Don't, Tommy! Oh, Gawd, Tommy, don't hurt me any more . . . he's gone to Tujunga Lake . . . he's got the map . . . the cache is somewhere near Tujunga Lake . . . I don't know any more . . . I don't want to be in this! Ooohhh — lemme outa here!'

He still held her, but more easily, as if he was actually trying to calm her down. And he was. He had no intention of letting her out of the cubbyhole looking like a dame that has just been ravaged.

'Okay, that's more like it,' he drawled. 'I get it. I suppose 'he' is Jerry Randell, huh? And he's got the map. A smart feller — how'd he get it? I'd like to know that.'

'Abe Craster mailed it to me,' sobbed Lita. 'Oh lemme outa here, will ya?'

'Mailed it to you?'

'Yeah, the guy had some stupid idea of concealing the whereabouts of this lousy map. I had to mail it to a cabin at Tujunga Lake — I mean the envelope inside. Now let me go . . . please . . . oh, God, don't go after Jerry Randell . . . he'll kill you!'

4

Jerry Randell drove his car up the dirt
road that led to Tujunga Lake and
wondered if this was really going to be the
end of his mission to destroy the cached
dope. He knew he had been lucky. And in
more ways than one because Lita Rossini
was some girl!

He had driven some fifteen miles out of
L.A. and all round the dirt road was thick
greenery, bushes, trees. But the telephone
company had strung wires up. He saw
them, fastened to convenient trees,
properly fixed and insulated. He thought
that was a cheap method of stringing
wire. He thought the wires must go to
some vacation cabin alongside the lake.
Well, if there was a buck to be earned, the
phone company would pause to pick it
up.

He figured to locate the dope and set
about destroying it. Then he would report
to Lieutenant Strang and after that Mr.

Roedeck, his client.

Jerry drove up the winding track as fast as the surface would allow and then, as he rolled down an incline, he saw the bright gleam of water just ahead between trees. So he was near the lake. He'd have to find the cabin. According to the address on the letter the cabin was called 'Southwest Cabin'. And it was somewhere near Tujunga Lake. Well, if the U.S. mailman could find it, so could a city slicker!

He saw the first of the cabins set just off the dirt road. He had to get out of the auto and go look at the place. It wasn't Southwest Cabin. Somebody had called it Shangri La. Jerry thought that had an odour and he returned to his car and drove on to the next and thought it would be hell if he had to circle the entire damned lake.

The next two places were elaborate cabins with phone wires sweeping down to stone chimneystacks, and when he approached on foot he saw they were occupied. One hadn't any name, but a couple sitting very close together on a canvas hammock shot him indignant looks. He got away from that porch fast. He drove along the dirt track and thought it got more like a goat trail with every hundred yards. Away to his right was the silvery sheen of the placid lake, fringed right down to the edge with tall trees and interlacing shrubs. He saw a canoe move slowly over the lake; heard sounds of a radio from somewhere. So the location wasn't entirely deserted.

In this way Jerry Randell went along the shore of the narrow, long lake and finally he found Southwest Cabin. At the moment of discovery he was standing about ten yards away from the porch, staring at the small cabin with the shuttered windows, and he could read the wood plate, on which was painted boldly: *Southwest Cabin.* So the mailman hadn't such a task after all!

Jerry returned to his auto and studied the map. He thought Abe Craster had been a careful guy because the drawing was explicit. The dope was cached in a disused silver mine tunnel which apparently ran into a hillock only twenty yards distant from the cabin.

Jerry stared around him and spotted the silver mine shaft. It made a hole in the incline behind the cabin and was fringed with thorn bushes. It probably wouldn't attract any interest except to those looking for it.

He got out of the auto; thrust the map into his billfold; walked up the incline again and passed the cabin. He figured it was empty. It was certainly one of the most isolated of all the cabins he had passed. There wasn't another place in sight and the wild greenery grew thick around the spot. Anybody who wanted a vacation up here must be fond of the lonely life. He bet the dead and unlovely Abe Craster hardly ever used the place.

Jerry Randell slowly approached the gap that had once been the pride and joy of some silver prospector. It seemed little more than a hole in the ground, barely high enough to admit a man bent double.

Jerry paused and thought swiftly about many things.

He didn't think about the cabin at all.

But there was a face at the window of the cabin and a pair of narrowed, glinting eyes that noted every movement that Jerry Randell made.

The cabin wasn't empty. And there was one window that was not shuttered. The face bobbed cautiously behind this pane of dirty glass.

Jerry Randell ducked and thrust his head and shoulders into the mouth of the hole. He wished he had brought a torch. But he would have to content himself with matches. The first few yards of the tunnel showed walls shored up with old timbers that were riddled with ant-holes. The whole damn place was anything but safe. It was anybody's guess why Abe Craster had picked on this spot to cache his consignment of dope. The workings of his mind would be his secret now.

Jerry moved about five yards into the hole and then struck a match because the daylight just about quit at this point. He still didn't see any boxes or packages that would indicate the valuable dope.

The match showed that the tunnel extended a lot longer into the hillock. But nothing in the shape of boxes! Only the grey rock and the dirt floor and some horrible species of fungus growing unnaturally out of the reach of sun and rain. Jerry moved further into the hole and he thought it was one hell of a place. As the mouth got further behind him, the confined space seemed more like a grave. But he went on grimly. He figured to go on until he located the dope or came up against the blank end of the shaft.

He had to use up three matches. He finally turned into a strange chamber cut in one side of the tunnel. It was barely five feet high, shored up with ancient timbers that looked like they would not continue with the useless task much longer. The most satisfactory part of the eerie scene was the pile of wood boxes, carefully built on an old stretch of waterproof canvas.

The cache!

Jerry bent over the stack; struck a fresh match and began a fast inspection. He whistled as he made a quick guess as to the value. It was not actually a big load; he could have placed the well-made boxes in the rear seating of his car. But the value must have been enormous. Abe had certainly hauled in a lot of stuff with one trick. Maybe he had bought the dope cheaply over the border. No wonder other hoods were interested!

The boxes were good quality plywood, seamless and with screwed-down lids, Jerry Randell figured that the dope would be packaged inside the boxes. There were no markings, nothing to indicate the origin of the stuff.

The match went out.

Jerry turned, several thoughts in his mind. Savagely, he figured he would have to burn the stuff there and then. He'd go out of the shaft and get some dry brushwood.

He'd drag it in — a lot of it — and pile it around the dope and then fire it and get out of the tunnel quickly. A fire in that confined space would certainly incinerate the dope and eventually cause the timbers to burn and then break. The result would be to bury the remains of the dope. In all it would be a dead loss for any hoods like Cal Owen and Rick Egler.

Jerry knew damned well that cocaine had a medicinal value and he was intending to destroy something worth a lot of dough. But this cache was not like something in a drug factory. Too many things could happen. It wasn't under control. It could he put to evil use, unlike the stuff stored by manufacturing druggists.

He moved down the shaft, head bent and shoulders clear of the tunnel sides. He wasn't using matches.

He figured he'd have to get busy. He'd get the job done and be finished with it.

Jerry Randell moved swiftly past the mouth of the hole, straightening his back thankfully as he cleared the tunnel.

He was utterly taken by surprise by the man who leaped at him with a heavy upraised stick. The chunk of wood swished through the air in a well-timed blow. Jerry got a frantic impression of an ugly, bearded face and a mouth twisted in a snarl — and then the club crashed down on his head.

Jerry Randell was just like any ordinary man; he could be taken by surprise and his skull wasn't built to stand vicious raps. He sagged.

He crumpled and lay in a heap at the mouth of the hole. The ugly character in shirt and pants stood over the fallen man and made strange chuckling noises. Then, picking Jerry up like a child, he carried him on his shoulder back to the cabin.

No one was around to notice anything. The door of Southwest Cabin closed again and a bolt rammed home. The gink with the bearded, dirty, ugly face threw Jerry Randell on the floor and stood over him for a minute. Then he went to a table; sat down and glanced angrily at the inch of liquid in a whisky bottle. He drank it off. He glared at the unconscious man again and began to make his idiotic noises. It went on for some time.

'Ah-ug-gug-gawk-sha-lum-yak-wah!'

The man seemed unable to talk. He also looked somewhat insane.

After the weird spiel was over, he went through Jerry Randell's pockets. He looked in the billfold. The only thing that meant anything to him was the small roll of bills. He took them and thrust them into his trouser pocket. Then he stuck the billfold back in Jerry's inside pocket.

The map meant nothing to him. And neither did the private detective licence.

But the man knew what was useful to him and what was not. He filched Jerry's cigarettes and lit one and smoked with obvious enjoyment.

Then, when the smoke was a hideously wet butt, he took some lengths of stout string from a locker and bound Jerry Randell's hands behind his back. He left his legs, figuring that was okay.

Jerry Randell first became aware of this cockeyed world again when he opened his eyes and stared at the face of a fox on the floor. The glassy eyes glared at him, inches from his face. Then Jerry shifted and knew the fox head was part of a skin rug on the floor. That brought back screwy memories. He last remembered the tunnel; this was a puzzling transition. He jerked, knew instantly his hands were tied; felt the cord bite deeply into his wrists. He rolled his head and focused screwed-up eyes on the queer bearded gink sitting at the table. Jerry took all this in for some seconds and then got the whole picture.

'Say, buster,' he muttered, 'what was the big idea? How do you fit in?'

A torrent of gibberish was hurled at him and the man rose and hit Jerry on the side of the head.

It was a nasty blow and sent the detective's brain reeling for some seconds. Jerry let the fog clear before talking again.

'So you're dumb, huh?' he muttered. 'Can't talk! But not deaf! You look crazy, but you're not quite. Wonder why you're here? I wonder if Abe Craster planted you here? Aw, hell, so what! How can I get out of this?'

The dumb man didn't offer any solution. Instead, he got up and swung another fist at Jerry that the shamus just avoided by ducking his head. That seemed to annoy the character and he spent some time uttering his horrible sounds.

'Threats, huh?' breathed Jerry. 'Okay. You can't talk but I can. I think you've got some sense and there's reason for you bein' here.' He paused; said clearly and loudly: 'Listen, bud, if you're waiting for

Abe Craster you'd better know he's dead.'
Jerry repeated: 'Abe's dead! Got it? Abe
Craster is dead.'

The gleam that shot into Hairyface's
eyes proved he understood. He shot
sounds at Jerry: 'Yag — wa — gurk!'

'I ain't lying,' said Jerry slowly. 'Abe
Craster is dead — so if he planted you
here you're on a dead horse.'

More: 'Gug — yak — sha — lap
— haa!'

'Take this rope off me,' snapped Jerry.
'The police are coming and you'll hit
grief. I'm a private detective — a shamus,
Understand? Abe Craster is dead and he
is in bad with the cops. Get this rope off
me!'

Hairyface shook his head. The refusal
was clear enough and indicated the man
understood simple instructions. But the
one-sided conversation did not get Jerry
Randell out of his fix!

They spent some time glaring at each
other. Then Hairyface shuffled through
the roll of bills he had taken off Jerry.
He seemed to find some delight in the
touch of the greenstuff. People with a lot

more intelligence have found the same delight, so the man wasn't queer in that respect!

'Rolled me, huh!' exclaimed Jerry Randell. 'Out of my billfold, too. And you can't read or count — I can see that the way you're handling those bills! I reckon Abe planted you here as a guardian — an' I bet you don't know what's in that tunnel. Yeah, that's the setup. This gink is waiting for Abe Craster to appear. And Abe intended to be here tomorrow morning — for the mailman. Maybe Hairyface was on hand to help him shift some of the consignment. Aw, the hell with it!'

His reflections were not getting him out of the fix. But he tried again.

'Look, feller, Abe Craster is dead. He can't get you any dough. The cops will be around here soon,'

The character rose again and smacked Jerry viciously on the side of his face. The punch left a little dull sound hanging momentarily in the air. Jerry felt the blow ram his senses out of this world. He just swayed and automatically closed his eyes.

Slowly his senses swam back again.

Two hundred yards away, down the dirt road, an auto approached the cabin and the driver cut his motor when he sighted Jerry Randell's car.

5

Lita Rossini felt bad. She leaned against the washbowl of the ladies' room and thought she might be sick. But she was not. Instead, she got control of herself. She rubbed her bruises and wondered if Tommy Berg had ruined her modelling for the next few days. She cursed the memory of him afresh.

She washed and dabbed her eyes where Tommy Berg had induced tears. She quickly powdered and applied lipstick. She adjusted something under her dress. She shoved everything back into her handbag. The sight of the .25 gun made her smile ironically. A lot of good it had been during the rumpus with Tommy Berg!

She made her decision. She wasn't turning into the art studio. She'd get an auto and hell up to Tujuna Lake.

She felt she owed it to Jerry Randell. He had helped her with the Craster death and she liked him. She didn't like the thought of Tommy Berg prowling up to the cabin at Tujunga Lake. Maybe Jerry could take care of the ruthless guy, but Jerry was entitled to a warning.

Unless she was too late!

She wasted not another second. With her urge of determination, she felt a lot better. She hurried out into the street and continued down until she came to a U-drive car depot. She went in and hustled up an already fast organisation. Luckily, she had enough dough in her handbag to make a deposit.

Only minutes later she drove out in a new Ford sedan. She could drive a Ford nicely. It was a good car and she sped through the L.A. streets, taking the roads up to Burbank and thence to Eagle Rock. Out of the built-up areas, she really put her neat little foot to the gas pedal.

She knew the roads to Tujunga, the little township a few miles before one got to the lake.

Lita went through this little part of Los Angeles and drove down the highway until she saw the indicator pointing the way to Tujunga Lake. She turned up the dirt road,

As yet she had little idea of what form her help to Jerry Randell might take. She mightn't find him. Tommy Berg might have lined a heater on him. Could be anything. All she had was an urge to get out there and warn Jerry that someone else knew about the map and the Tujunga Lake location.

The bumpy track slowed her but all the same she kept moving fast. The first of the cabins came in sight. She knew she needed to sight Jerry Randell's auto to place him. She didn't have to look for Southwest Cabin.

When she did sight Jerry's auto in the distance, she also saw the second car parked not so far off. She had not seen the car before, but she had a hunch it belonged to Tommy Berg. So he had caught up with Jerry!

Her first instinct was to brake her Ford. Then she reacted and fed more gas. She steered off the track; took the car up the grassy slope and then, when she could go no further because of thick thorn bushes, she halted and set the handbrake firmly. She got out of the auto, clutching her handbag. She stared at the small cabin, the two cars and the general atmosphere of silence. What was going on?

At that moment, as if in answer to her questions, the door of the cabin opened and two men walked out. One was Tommy Berg and the other was Jerry Randell. The two didn't emerge exactly like pals! Far from it. Tommy Berg had a gun rammed in Jerry's back. And Lita could see that Jerry's hands were tied behind him.

That wasn't the lot. The two men hardly got off the porch when another figure appeared at the cabin door — a big lurching man who, even at a distant view, was clearly in a helluva rage. But a motion of Tommy Berg's gun kept the third man at bay,

Lita didn't get the entire setup. But her first impressions were that Jerry had not located the dope. Secondly, she wondered how come Jerry's hands got tied behind his back and, thirdly, where did the big bearded man come in?

She stopped trying to puzzle out the setup and figured she had to do something and this time she would use her .25. She knew how to shoot. She had bought the little heater and taken lessons at shooting. That had been recently in reaction to a sex-maniac scare in L.A

Lita remembered how Tommy Berg had ill-treated her and she felt she could cheerfully pump a few slugs into him. But the little gun was no good except at close quarters.

She heard Tommy Berg cursing. She saw the bearded man moving slowly after the two men. He was keeping his distance but the gun wasn't stopping him entirely.

Tommy Berg decided something drastic had to he done. His gun moved and cracked. The big man suddenly fell to his knees. At that moment Jerry Randell leaped away.

He had got some yards when Tommy Berg yelled him to stop. Jerry went on at the fastest stride he could muster. Tommy Berg made the mistake of yelling out that he would shoot. Jerry Randell figured he would not. And, of course, he was right.

Tommy Berg did not know where he would find the map or the cached dope and he couldn't kill the other man until he knew something definite.

Lita screeched: 'Up here, Jerry!'

He saw her; swerved towards her. Tommy Berg launched into a fast stride, his gun swinging in his fist. He left behind Hairyface, who stirred and actually got to his feet and lumbered off into the bushes.

Lita Rossini aimed her little heater at Tommy Berg and waited coolly. But all the same she fired from a good distance for a little gun of that sort. The slug whistled over Tommy Berg's head. He slowed, raised his own heater. In his rage he threw a slug at Lita Rossini. It was a wild shot and missed. In fact, it hit one of the side windows of the new Ford and made a jagged star in the side of the glass!

Tommy Berg had lost ground and Jerry Randell could run like a sprinter. He made straight for Lita's auto and piled in without wasting a second. Lita had sensed the play and she was inside the car simultaneously. She stabbed the engine to life; shot the auto away in a quick circle and headed down the slope to the track.

Tommy Berg couldn't stop their getaway with a gun and he knew the disadvantages of attracting attention by a number of gunshots. There were folks in other cabins not so far away. Of course, people went duck-shooting, but there was a difference in the sound of the guns.

He tore back to his own car. He figured he'd even up. If Jerry Randell had Abe Craster's map, he wanted it!

He did not notice that the bearded man had disappeared!

Jerry Randell braced himself as Lita Rossini drove crazily down the track. He stuck it for some fast seconds and then he thought the time had come for him to be rid of the cords Hairyface had slung around his wrists. He said so to Lita.

'Look, baby, I got a pocket-knife. Get it out and cut these damned bindings!'

'Don't you want to get away? I'll have to stop the car.'

'Sure you'll have to stop — you'd be good if you could drive and cut me free at the same time! Don't worry about Berg — that's the guy you know, ain't it? He dropped the hint that was his monicker. I got my gun still and if he shows up he'll run into trouble.'

Lita obeyed. She halted the auto and, reaching into Jerry Randell's pocket, found the folding knife. From then on it was only the work of seconds to slice through the cords on his wrists.

He didn't even rub his wrists. He heaved out his gun and stared back through the rear window. As yet there was no sign of Tommy Berg.

'I'm gettin' out,' he snapped. 'Drive this car among some bushes where it won't be easily seen and then come back to me. I'll be over here.'

With a few lithe leaps he stationed himself among the thick bushes. The last thing Lita saw was the gun poking out. Then she shot the car forward again.

She went down the dirt road only twenty yards when she discovered the perfect concealment for the auto. She rolled the car into the natural nook and then jumped out and made her way back to where she had left Jerry Randell.

Before she got to him, she heard a gun

crack and the revving of an auto engine as someone backed hastily. Then she was beside Jerry.

'That was your pal!' he snapped. 'He drove down the track fast as hell!'

'Don't call him my pal!' rapped Lita, and she related swiftly how Tommy Berg had trapped her and extracted the information from her.

'I'll even with that louse,' cursed Jerry. 'I'll teach him to muss you up! Just wait!'

'What happened to you?' Lita laid a hand on his sleeve; stared at his grey, narrowed eyes. 'Who tied you?'

'I found the dope in the silver mine tunnel as the drawing indicates. No one would go into that hole in the ground if they didn't know. I was coming out when that galoot rapped me on the head. I passed out and came back into this cuckoo world inside the cabin, and Hairyface was over me. He'd tied me and taken my dough, but I notice he didn't take the map or anythin' else. Hairyface is dumb and I guess he can't read. I think Abe stuck him in the cabin to keep an eye on the cached dope — only that galoot doesn't know the nature of the stuff in that shaft.'

'I saw that bearded guy. You mean he is really dumb — can't talk?'

'Yeah, that's it. He just makes the most goddam awful sounds.' Jerry peered closely through the greenery. 'I wonder where Tommy Berg is?'

Lita glanced around the leafy surroundings and thought a shot could glance out from almost anywhere.

'Let's get out of this!' she urged.

'You forgettin' about that dope? I've got to destroy it.'

'Tommy Berg doesn't know where it is.'

'Maybe. He knows it's somewhere around though. And he might grab hold of Hairyface — although I'm damned if I know how he'll get any sense out of that lunkhead.'

'Well, there you are. Let's get out of this, Jerry!'

'Nope. Look, baby, this ain't your plate of meat. Get back to the auto an' drive away. Me — I got an auto up there to collect in any case. Say, where did you get the Ford?'

'I hired it.'

'The window is shot to hell.'

'You're tellin' me! I guess I'll have to foot the bill.'

'Sure, well, get goin'.'

'I'm not leavin' you.' She caught his eyes with a defiant expression in her green ones.

He chuckled. 'Look, this isn't a goddam comic strip. It's — '

He broke off because a rustling noise had sounded just ahead.

'Keep ya damned head down!' he hissed. 'That stupid bum is comin' after us! Looks like he wants to mix it! Goddam him. He'll try to kill me and get the map.'

'Looks like it,' gulped Lita.

Jerry Randell crouched low, only his narrowed eyes moving, wary, like a cat on the hunt. He appreciated that the other guy was pretty ruthless and being brave might just be a means of stopping a slug. A man only needed only one slug between the eyes to be on his way.

'You told him I had the map?' he muttered.

'Yeah, He squeezed it out of me — literally!' snapped the girl.

'The map, huh? Sure, he doesn't know where the dope is cached until he gets the map. And he ain't the only one. I guess Cal Owen and Rick Egler and a few more L.A. hoods would like to see this map. Okay.'

And Jerry Randell took the sheet of paper out of his billfold and began tearing it into very small bits. Lita watched him and listened for further sounds of anyone approaching — a twin task. Jerry soon had a handful of small bits of paper. They might have done very well for a wedding, but nothing much else! He swung his hand and the fistful of confetti scattered far and wide into the air.

'Okay,' murmured Jerry grimly, 'only you and me know where to find that dope.'

'Why did Abe Craster bother to make a drawing?' asked Lita. 'That's been on my mind.'

'One of these careful ginks, maybe. Or more like it, he didn't trust his own memory. And it could be he had thought of selling the stuff to some other crooked big shot — and such a gink might need a map. Seeing Abe's dead, we'll never really know.'

Lita glanced at the odd bit of paper lying a yard away. 'That's the end of the map, anyway. The guy who can fit that together — or find the bits — will be very smart.'

Without warning the figure of a man came pushing through the tangled bushes. Lita and Jerry dropped out of sight as if by magic. The man was Tommy Berg and he had not seen the other two.

He blundered past, missing the two he wanted in a way that is possible when men hunt each other in dense foliage. Jerry Randell rose at the right moment and went after the man. He moved with an incredible silence, like an Indian almost. Lita stayed down behind the bush, instinctively and fearfully, her heart beating so loudly she was sure Tommy Berg could hear it!

Jerry Randell got the drop on his man suddenly and savagely. He saw an advantage in slipping through a clear space, and then he leaped.

He landed on the other man's back. His gun was rammed into his shoulder holster. He figured to fight this out another way. He had a brute feeling to smash this man for the way he had treated Lita Rossini. That was about all.

6

It was one of those fights that snarl into animal fury right from the word go and the gentlemanly rules of ring-fighting are all shot to hell. Jerry's crashing body rammed him so hard initially that Tommy Berg dropped his gun. In a second it was kicked yards away by scuffling shoes. Tommy Berg was a man with a truckload of roughhouse tricks for all his city slicker ways. He twisted and kicked furiously at Jerry Randell's shins. Jerry took one rap and then hopped clear. Tommy Berg, clear now of the other's wrestling grip, slammed out a wickedly low punch. Jerry avoided it with a twist and the blow merely scraped along his belly. Then Jerry planted two steady punches that rocked Tommy Berg back against a tree trunk.

He launched himself at the man and grabbed him. He lifted Tommy Berg away from the tree trunk and then rammed him back. The man's head contacted with the tree with a dull sickly sound. Jerry Randell did it again. Tommy Berg's arms lay limply at his side, a sure indication that his brainpan was reeling. Jerry had the man neat. He could have bust him up. He could have killed him except that, even in his rage, he knew that homicide wasn't yet in the book.

After the third bashing against the tree bole, Tommy Berg's eyes were contorted slits and he was becoming a weight in Jerry's grip. Jerry held him up with one iron-hard hand. He slapped him around the chops with his other fist. Tommy Berg's mouth bubbled blood and saliva. He didn't look so handsome now. Behind the two combatants, Lita Rossini screamed: 'Give him hell, Jerry! Give him hell!'

Jerry let his brute desires have a workout on the luckless crook. He did not need Lita's advice. He just remembered that Tommy Berg had manhandled the girl.

When he had finished, Tommy Berg sprawled among the roots of the tree and looked just as twisted and ugly. Jerry stepped back, hunted through his pocket for his handkerchief and slowly began to wipe his hands. He calmed; got the essentials of this scene. He was acting like a goddamn fool. He had stopped Tommy Berg's man-hunt — that was surely enough, No need for any more. The guy had lost his gun and without that he wasn't killing anyone! And there wasn't any chance of Berg getting the map now — although the crook hardly knew that!

Lita edged closer and stared momentarily at the fallen man. Then she kicked suddenly, her shoe catching the man in the ribs.

'Cut it out!' snarled Jerry.

'Yeah? That louse nearly twisted a lump out of me — remember?'

'Sure, but cut it out. He's had enough. He'll have to get the hell out of here when he comes round. He can't win. We dump him in his auto and see him get goin'. Then I reckon I'll attend to that lousy dope. I still aim to fire it. I could call the cops, if I got near a phone, but the hell with it. I want to burn the hellish stuff!'

'Okay. I'll help you.'

Jerry Randell carried the other man out

of the greenery and made his way up the track. After some twenty yards, Tommy Berg stirred. Jerry figured he was sick of carrying the heavy lunk and so he set him down on the earth and waited. Tommy Berg came back into this world and apparently did not think much of it for he snarled and spat and twisted his face.

'Get on your damned legs,' snapped Jerry. 'You're goin' back to your heap an' then you're lightin' out.'

The other just sneered so Jerry reached out and hauled the guy up. Tommy Berg was on his feet but very unsteadily. Jerry jabbed him into forward movement.

'For hell's sake get goin'! You can't win a damned thing! Get smart and get into your auto and beat it — punk!'

Tommy Berg had the pride of a big guy and he hated the realisation that he had been whipped. He shot vicious glances at Jerry and Lita but kept stumbling on. He didn't try any more fighting; he knew it was futile. His head was just a hell of fiery torment, and blood was seeping down one side. He had an ugly abrasion where skin and hair had been scraped away from the back of his head. He was in a shocking state.

In this way he reached his car, parked further up the track, and slid in. He started the engine, and as he rolled the car slowly forward he spat some crude epithet at Jerry and Lita. And then he was on his way. They waited until the sound of his auto died away.

'Okay. I wonder if Hairyface is badly hurt?'

'I saw him get up and beat it,' said Lita.

Jerry exclaimed: 'The hell you did! I'll have to watch for that moron!'

'And I ought to go get my Ford,' said Lita. 'I'm getting worried about that car. I have to pay for all damage!'

'I'll go with you,' decided Jerry, 'just in case Tommy Berg is still snoopin' around. If he is he's a fool and don't know when to quit. Sure, you'd better bring the auto up to the cabin — near my car. We're only wastin' a few more minutes.'

They went back along the track, where the tall trees and interlaced bushes formed a façade on both sides, and they walked along arm-in-arm. Lita Rossini started it. She had begun to have admiration for this man and she liked to feel his arms around her. She had just gotten out of a bad fix and she wanted the tangible comfort of his arms!

They got the Ford out of the shady nook and Jerry drove it back and parked it near his own beside the cabin. Then they got out.

'Okay,' he said grimly, 'now that you're here you can help me burn that blasted dope. And keep an eye open for Hairyface. Where the devil did that guy get to, anyway? I figured he stopped Tommy Berg's slug!'

'He did,' said Lita, 'but it seems like he's plenty tough. Anyway, he's disappeared.'

'Just to make sure, I'll take a look in the cabin,' decided Jerry.

But the cabin was empty. He came down off the porch and stared around at the brooding screens of greenery. Could be the bearded man was waiting with revenge as his intent.

'Aw, let's get up to that silver mineshaft,' snapped Jerry.

As they walked up the slope, Lita exclaimed: 'Oh, well, this is sure some change from modeling!'

'It ain't my usual line of detective work,' Jerry grunted. 'So don't get the wrong idea. I contact bad 'uns, sure, in my line of work, but I don't usually hell around like this.'

He led her up to the gaping hole of the old silver mine tunnel. They paused while he said: 'This is it. This is the hole where Abe Craster figured his dope would be safe until he arranged for disposal.'

'You been in there?' Lita peered in distastefully.

'Sure. Goes right way back.'

'I don't like it. I'm not going in there.'

'Okay, baby, you stick around outside an' keep that .25 heater prominent.'

Jerry Randell first grabbed at some dry, loose brushwood lying nearby, and then dragged it into the tunnel. He disappeared down the dark hole, leaving Lita at the mouth. She stared around, a trifle apprehensive now that she was once more alone. She had swift, jagged thoughts, wondering why she was mixed up in this circus! All this because she had innocently gone to Abe Craster's apartment!

She slid her gun out of her handbag; held it loosely. She shot one more wary glance around and then stared into the ugly hole in the ground that had swallowed Jerry.

There was some kind of fascination about the silent gaping hole in the earth, and she just stared, conjuring up wild fancies. What if Jerry didn't return! What if the roof caved in! Maybe he'd get stuck!

She couldn't be blamed for not hearing or sensing the approach of the big bearded man. He came up like he was doubling for an Indian tracker. He moved with extraordinary stealth for a man of his weight.

His arms went around Lita Rossini and that was the first thing she knew about it. It was also too late to utter a scream because the man wasn't as crazy as he looked and he had promptly thrust a big, dirty hand over the girl's mouth.

The next instant, despite her struggles, Lita found herself being dragged over the ground. She dropped her gun with the handbag. It lay forlornly on the ground only yards from the tunnel mouth. The bearded man increased his pace, carrying the girl with little effort. The thick bushes and interlaced weeds closed on them. All that remained to mark their passing was the waving of violently-disturbed bushes.

The man carried her through a thickly-wooded part of land and, reaching a hollow, dumped her on the ground.

He held her down. His hairy visage worked and strange sounds came from his mouth. He was trying to talk to her.

None of it made any sense. Lita hugged the earth — scared to hell and high heaven, and wished she could summon energy to fight her way free from this maniac.

His arms gripped her, jerked her upright, twisted her round to face him. She was brought flat against him. Her green eyes widened and widened, fear and horror touching off stark lights in them. She fought, strength now returning. She saw the bloody patch on his shoulder and knew he had only been punctured by Tommy Berg's slug. Apparently the brute wasn't feeling it much.

She slashed at his face with long, wicked fingernails. He jerked his head back, but continued to hold her like a bear. His lips showed unpleasantly red in the middle of his hairy mouth. His breath suggested he had pus in his veins instead of blood. It was like wrestling with some obscene animal . . . She began to sob. Her strength was no match for this godforsaken louse.

Sudden inspiration came to her. She raised her right foot, brought it down sharply. The sharp heel of her shoe dug into the bridge of his foot. Even as he gave a yell of protest, she did it again — then again. His grip slackened amid a torrent of gasps and whimpers at the agony in his foot.

Wrenching herself free, Lita turned and ran . . .

7

Jerry Randell came rushing out of the silver mine tunnel!

He came out like someone startled. He was yelling at the top of his voice and the words vibrated in the air before he realised Lita Rossini was nowhere in sight.

'Lita, the damned dope has vanished — ' Then he jarred to a halt in more ways than one; the girl wasn't at the tunnel mouth!

He was a quickly reacting man; he wouldn't have been the owner and one-manband of a detective agency if he lacked fast thinking. He'd already assimilated the unpleasant and incredible fact that the boxes of dope had vanished — he could, in fact, guess how. Now Lita!

He made a sudden angry dart across the ground and picked up the girl's gun and handbag. Instinctively he dropped the gun inside and zipped it up. If he'd had any doubt, this clinched it.

Hairyface had the girl! Obviously, the bearded wretch was responsible because only he knew about the tunnel.

Jerry Randell slipped out his own gun and raced up to the fringe of interlacing bushes, thorns, weeds and trees. He dived in and then slowed, bedevilled by uncertainly.

Lita could be anywhere!

It was a dreadful note. But he had to find her, and he had to find Hairyface because that wretch alone knew the present whereabouts of the dope!

He raced into the thick lacing of greenery; stared grimly ahead through the mellow light. When he stopped to listen, as he frequently did, a thousand small rustling sounds came to his ears. Then he plunged on and circled to the right a bit. He hadn't a clue and he felt sour and mean. He pushed into a chunk of wild laurel and when branches whipped springily at him, he punched them viciously like a man who is plenty mad. With every yard he became less the shrewd shamus and more like a savage hunter.

Then he heard the scream from somewhere ahead. He jerked in that direction, legs impelling him like some great cat, hands clawing out, one clutching his gun. He sprang over the uneven earth with terrific speed. He heard another scream — knew it for a woman.

And then, in seconds, a curtain of green leaves burst apart and Lita Rossini ran blindly forward. She did not even see Jerry so great was her hysteria. He had to catch her flying arms and swing her back abruptly. Even then she stared unseeingly at him, her teeth clenched and her mouth a twisted gash.

He held her grimly; even shook her. He could not let her go — and all the time he was well aware that the man he wanted was making off. He couldn't leave Lita in her present panic.

Gradually, she calmed as he held her. He noticed sombrely the tears in her dress, the horrible imprints of bruises on her face and arms and neck. She quit sobbing after he'd held her some minutes. She was a frightened woman and she wanted comforting; she laid her cheek on his chest. He held her up. She was just about limp.

'All right, what did he do to you?'

'Oh, Jerry, I can't tell you!' she wailed. 'It's too horrible what he tried! He's a monster . . . just a crazy swine! Get me outa here, Jerry, before I go outa my mind!'

'I'll get you to that cabin — might find something there so you can clean up. You need a sit down, baby.'

There was nothing else for it but to take Lita Rossini back to the cabin and take it easy. They got in because the door was unlocked. She sank down to a seat; took her handbag from his hands. She wiped her face grimly as if to clear away rotten memories. After a moment of this, she said:

'Okay. Go on and get your work done firing that dope.'

He took time out for a curt laugh.

'That's good, baby. What you don't know is that the dope is missing.'

She raised her face. 'What?'

'Gone! Vamoosed! The whole damn lot

— all those boxes. Hairyface was evidently busy while we played tag with Tommy Berg. He must have worked fast. That goddam slug ain't hurtin' him much, I guess.'

'You — you found that out!' Lita almost stuttered.

'Yeah, an' then when I came hellin' out of that tunnel you had gone and left only your handbag! Gee, you an' that damned handbag! That's the second time I've picked it up!'

Lita shivered. 'I seem to be hitting nothing hut grief. Not that that's anything new in my life. My curves have been getting me into trouble all my life. Now this!' She lowered bitter eyes to her torn and ruined nylons.

He came closer; laid a hand on her shoulder. 'You feel a bit better? Look, stay in this cabin — lock the door after me. I want to scout around. Maybe I'll find some sign that'll lead me to those stupid boxes of dope. Or maybe I'll run into that crazy slob.'

'Don't leave me again!'

'I got to!' he protested. 'This big slob is

maybe getting miles away. Look, bolt the door. Make yourself some coffee — you might find some in a locker. There's a gas ring with a pressure container.'

'Okay, you big lug.' She flashed him a glance. 'But hurry back.'

'Yeah. Hang onto that .25, baby. And lock the door.'

Jerry raced away from the cabin and thought this hell-around couldn't have taken place at one of the other cabins because there were neighbouring shacks in sight inhabited by vacationers. He sliced into the green wood again, striding steadily from one vantage point to another, his gun in his hand, He glanced around sharply all the time for signs of the lurking Hairyface. There was a chance the guy had beat it. But maybe he was still hanging around. Maybe he was guarding the boxes of dope. Anything could give with a nutty character like this. It was a good bet the man did not know anything about the nature of the boxes. Abe Craster would have kept silent on the value, that was a sure thing. Abe would have strung this lunkhead along with some tale. Abe probably understood him. In a way, it was a pity Abe wasn't around to converse with the ape!

So that was a helluva note — a screwball knowing where to find a cache of dope valued at probably well over a hundred grand. That was its underground market value; its medicinal value was probably a lot less. If he, Jerry Randell, could find it right now its medicinal value would be zero!

Jerry strode on, passing clearings and jumping small holes, and as the time passed his thoughts were pretty sombre. It was hitting him hard as a poker on the head that Hairyface was not going to be found easily and the dope was probably cunningly hidden.

Now there wasn't even a map! Just a gink who couldn't talk!

Jerry Randell thrust back to the clearing that fringed the lakeshore. He walked carefully back to the silver mine shaft and searched around for any sign that might indicate where Hairyface had taken the boxes of dope. There was a trail of footprints but they just made a mess around the tunnel mouth and then faded into nothing on hard earth so many yards away. They only indicated that the dumb lunkhead had proceeded to the right of the cabin. He had gone up to the fringe of the lake.

Jerry spent a lot of time searching around until he realized it was hopeless.

With that he tramped back to the cabin and knocked on the door and snapped to Lita:

'Open up — it's me, Jerry.'

The door shot open and a soft, desirable girl in clean, lovely clothes was in his arms.

'As if I didn't know!' she exclaimed. 'I've been watching you through a crack in a shutter. How'd you like my new dress, huh? Stockings, too!'

She had cleaned up and was dressed in a summery length of cotton spotted with gay polka dots. It fitted wicked hips snugly. He gazed in astonishment at sheer nylons that moulded to the swell of her legs. She saw his scrutiny; smiled impishly. Then he noted the new make-up; the ton of insolent lipstick.

'You look new!' he said. 'Where'd you get the dress?'

'It was in the cabin — and so were the stockings. In the bedroom. Seems like Abe did use this cabin once — with a popsy. He must have bought her some new clothes for services rendered because it looks like she left her old ones. Anyway, they're very useful and I feel a hundred per cent better.'

'You look it.'

They embraced for a while, then Jerry told her how he had searched everywhere without success,.

'Oh, let's beat it out of here,' she argued. 'That nut will probably forget where he parked the dope. Let's move. I gotta job to attend.'

He went to a shuttered window and stared at the shafts of bright sunlight slanting through. He glanced at his watch and thought it was incredible that it was not yet midday. So much had flashed across the setup that morning! The receipt of the letter — the appearance of Hairyface — Tommy Berg's attempt to get the map — now the disappearance of the dope!

'Forget about your job,' he snapped. 'For today, at any rate. One thing is pretty sure, that dope is around this locality somewhere. Hairyface is like some stupid dog — he's transferred his home someplace else because folks are interferin'. Evena big guy can't carry all those boxes without making a number of trips — and so I figure the dope won't be moved again. I'm stickin' here until I locate it. And you can help, baby!'

She stared at him. 'Me? How?'

'By stickin' around. If you're around, Hairyface will come nosin' back again. That's when I'll get him.'

Angrily, she placed her hands on hips. 'You want me to act like a decoy?'

'I'll see you don't get hurt,' he protested.

'I've *been* hurt!' she flared. 'Look, Jerry, this circus is nothing to me! You an' this damned dope! I don't give a cuss about it. And now you're setting me up as a decoy!'

He whipped to her and took her into his arms. He kissed her fast and she melted willingly. He brought his mouth back a few inches, rapped: 'You won't get hurt. I'll see to that. Just don't go away yet, baby. Anyway, the day is bust-up in any case so far as your modelling is concerned. Surely you're entitled to a day off now and then?'

'You don't know Erlich.' She gave a short laugh. 'Okay, you lug. I'll stick around. But I swear to hell I'll scream the goddam wood down the moment I sight that hairy ape!'

He grinned. 'You scream, baby. I'll deal with the lunkhead.'

He stood beside one of the shuttered windows for some time, staring through a crack. There was silence all around the clearing. He went to the window that was not shuttered and, cautiously, spent some time watching from there. But it was no dice. Hairyface was seemingly in no hurry to slouch back to the cabin. But Jerry Randell felt grimly sure the lunkhead would return. He'd come back like some animal drawn to the scene of a kill.

It was an irritating hiatus, and as the tempo changed he became restless, moving senselessly around the cabin, from the bedroom to the living room. Lita Rossini had made coffee, sure enough. The cabin contained all the necessary gear to make the brew. She handed him a cup and he realized he was getting hungry.

'How long do we stick here?' she asked. 'You forgetting about Tommy Berg?'

'I'm not,' he answered grimly. 'I know darned well he'll be back in the play soon as he gets over that beatin'.'

'All this because of some dope,' Lita muttered.

'Baby, that stuff is worse than dynamite. When Abe Craster brought that stuff into Los Angeles County, he brought a heap of grief.'

Later he left the cabin and hid himself in the tangled bushes that fringed the wood only yards away, and he watched Lita as she walked slowly and warily around the cabin and then mounted the porch again. If Hairyface was snooping, he hoped the sight of the girl would draw him. Right now he could think of no other way to locate the dope. Only the dumb lunkhead knew where it was hidden. The guy had certainly worked hard to shift the boxes in the limited time, but undoubtedly he had done it. It was some feat considering he had a gun-wound. Even a nick in the shoulder was some handicap in shifting a number of boxes!

Jerry Randell watched the cabin, the edge of the tangled wood and the lakeshore only so many yards away from the vacation cabin. Silence softened the air; the rustle of branches and the chirping of birds was a hardly audible background. He felt his growing hunger and realized he was missing lunch. He cursed Hairyface, and he cursed the fooling around that had taken place after Tommy Berg had been beaten up. A quicker return to the mineshaft might have caught the dumb guy in the act of moving the dope. It was tantalizing to know that the dope could be hidden somewhere in the area of wood and lake and yet still be out of reach.

A long time passed in this watchful manner and Jerry Randell felt mighty sour. Maybe his hunch about Hairyface was all wrong. Maybe the cluck was getting out of it but fast!

Jerry waited, tight-mouthed. He figured it was bad psychology to suppose the dumb guy was running away from his precious cache. He'd bet Hairyface would stick around to see no one stumbled on the new hiding-place!

The sun's brassy orb was right overhead when sudden distant shouts impinged on Jerry's ears.

He whipped around at the angry, distant bawling voices and knew instantly they were not vacationers!

8

Jerry Randell started into an urgent run, holding his gun forward, ready to spit a fast slug in defence or anger.

It was hard to analyse the quality of the shouting voices, but he knew two or three men were involved and it was a savage hullabaloo. Then, as quickly as it had come, it ceased. Jerry Randell went on, a fixed idea of the direction of the row in his mind. He jumped and leaped through the forest, slipping lithely around trees, pushing swiftly through the thinnest clumps of bushes.

He got a glimpse of three struggling men carrying something that writhed and uttered unearthly sounds. It was enough to make Jerry pause and he darted behind a tree. The photographic impression had conveyed a lot to him. In the split second he'd seen Tommy Berg's big back and the unpleasant faces of Cal Owen and Rick Egler. And they had hold of Hairyface and were carrying him off like a protesting steer going to the slaughter-house!

After the first pause, Jerry Randell moved on again. In a few flashes of thought he knew the setup. Tommy Berg had scrammed, and had driven to the nearest phone. There were plenty among the vacation cabins. So the smart guy had phoned Cal Owen and Rick Egler, throwing in his information because he wanted their help. It seemed like the two hoods had torn up to the lakeside in an auto, and now, with the devil's own luck, had blundered into Hairyface at the first moment. Tommy Berg knew the lunkhead knew where the dope was cached.

Tommy Berg didn't know the stuff had been moved. But that hardly mattered, seeing he and his pals had hold of the man who really knew where to locate the dope!

The three men ahead were swiftly plunging through the wood and the carcase they were carrying had quit writhing and moaning. One of the hoods had put Hairyface to sleep. Jerry came after them and, when a chance came, raised his gun. He squinted and squeezed the trigger. Even as the heater barked its little tune, he knew it was a lousy business. He was a law-abiding dick and he couldn't hell around killing men.

The thought had effect on his shooting in an unconscious manner. But his reluctance to kill didn't stop the slug or minimise the bark of the heater.

The bullet dug fiendishly into the earth right at the feet of Rick Egler. The crack of the gun made the hoods jump for cover. There was an ungodly scramble and Hairyface was thrown around like a bundle of old scrap. But the whole party dived into a hole over which a hush spread covering branches. The next instant a gun threw a barking slug at Jerry Randell.

He jumped to the cover of a tree bole because he had a hunch the hoods might not have his scruples about murder.

But he snapped off another shot because he was seething with rage. He threw the slug into the sheltering bush and then hoped to the devil it had not bitten into any vital part of Hairyface's body! It might be too bad if the lunkhead passed out. On the other hand, would it? The dope would just stay hidden and that would be the end of it.

Right now such conjectures were out. Three hoods had hold of Abe Craster's dumb guardian and they were the sort of men who could prise information out of a fossilized fish!

Jerry saw a frantic rustling of the bush covering the hole. He got a momentary glimpse of the men beating it from their front line. He pumped another shot at them and wondered if the gunplay would attract any vacationers. Probably not. Hopeful characters were always pot-shotting at ducks around these rural retreats.

Jerry moved after the palookas. He didn't see what he could do except hope they'd drop Hairyface.

But it was not to be. Jerry Randell could not close up and grapple with three hoods and as this was not a B-grade western movie he could not pick the men off with his heater in the accepted manner. The cops called the killing of other people homicide until a guy could prove self-defence. Proving that wasn't so easy. Killing was not so easy as some people figured; a man had to have the lust to kill. And anybody built that way should be certified!

The scramble through the wood was rough on clothes urgent and jerky. It ended abruptly when Jerry Randell saw the three hoods bundling the unconscious body of Hairyface into an auto.

In his rage, Jerry let the crooks have a couple more shots. One splintered the rear window of the car but apparently did not hit anything human. The other ploughed into the roof and stayed there. Then the auto lurched into motion, shooting off like something catapulted!

In a second Jerry Randell was just a rage-filled, helpless man standing on the edge of the track watching the disappearing auto. He rammed his gun into the shoulder holster. He balled his fists and then swung around. He broke into a fast run and went along the track towards Abe Craster's cabin and the two cars.

Lita Rossini was on the cabin porch as

he ran up and she took a few steps to meet him.

'Oh, Jerry, I heard those shots!'

'Yeah! Tommy Berg has got hold of Hairyface! Just his lousy luck! I searched all over for that slob and could not hit on him, but these damned crooks blundered right onto him. Tommy Berg was with Cal Owen and Rick Egler.'

He shot out a few more explanations that put her wise, and then grabbed her arm. 'You drive your Ford and I'll take my car. We're gettin' after those birds!'

He slammed the cabin door shut. They went to their cars, dived in and started them forward.

Lita Rossini was mighty glad in one way to be leaving Tujunga Lake, but she wasn't so happy about the prospect of a chase after three determined hoods.

But the way it played out there wasn't any chase. True, Jerry Randell drove very fast down the dirt road until it reached the highway. He rolled onto the main road and fed gas to the engine and let the car rip for some miles in the direction of L.A. Lita Rossini kept her Ford on his tail and then when he braked she slowed her car. He halted, jumped out and came to her side window with a grim expression on his firm jaw and grey eyes.

'Those birds have just that much head start. Maybe they ain't even on this highway. Might have branched off. I can't see 'em, anyway, and we've passed a few cars. Baby, we're lost off. Those palookas have Hairyface.'

'If they're banking on making him talk, that's very funny!' observed Lita.

He glanced at his watch; then brushed moss and dirt from his trousers. 'Let's get back to town. Maybe I'll bring the cops in on it,'

'We're going back, sure thing,' said Lita. 'I've got to hand this auto in and pay for damage!'

'I'll take care of that,' he said, and he did, when they got back to Los Angeles. Then he drove her to his office on Slausen Street. 'You're not going to Erlichs today,' he said. 'Take the day off, baby.'

She looked around the small office, noted the battered desk, the phone, the dagger sticking in the desk, the fan on the top of a steel filing-cabinet, the old-fashioned safe and the big wide window that looked down on busy Slausen.

'So this is where the crime-buster hangs out,' she remarked.

'Yeah. I sleep in a room upstairs and eat just about anywhere.'

'Why mention sleep? And why look at me with the speculative eye? You're off-beam, brother. I'm more hungry than tired.'

Jerry Randell placed a hand on the phone, hesitated and frowned. 'I ought to call the cops about that dope!' He took his hand off the instrument. 'Maybe I'll give it another few more hours.'

They went out to a little restaurant only a few doors away and wasted no time on a satisfactory lunch. Then back to Jerry's office. He went up to his room and cleaned up, changed his shirt and necktie and socks. He was busy when Lita Rossini came up the stairs and walked in with an inquiring look. She sat before a dressing-mirror and examined her appearance critically.

He came up behind her and placed hands round the nape of her neck.

Then she wriggled free. 'This ain't the time! Don't get me going, brother! Gee, I don't know why I should fall for a lug like you!'

He grinned. 'Don't fight against it, baby!'

In spite of her attractions, he began thinking about his mission to get hold of the cached dope. He went down to his office still deep in thought. He stood over the phone and wondered if he should slick the cops onto the task of finding the hidden dope. A squad of bulls, probing and tramping all over the lakeside, might easily unearth the missing stuff.

Jerry Randell wasn't exactly a Boy Scout and he saw no reason why he should push all his information into the hands of the cops and leave them to grab credit. He wanted the credit for finding the dope. He was in business and a guy couldn't afford to pass up factors that would add to his reputation.

So he walked away from the phone!

Half an hour later Jerry Randell and

Lita Rossini went out. They went along to the bar room on the corner of Pico and Lincoln Boulevard — the joint called Joe's Place where Lita had last seen Tommy Berg. They didn't expect to find the guy sitting drinking ale! He would be helping Cal Owen and Rick Egler make a dumb guy talk — some chore!

Jerry and Lita just vaguely hoped for a lead. It was better than sitting around. When a dog loses the scent it just sniffs around until it picks it up again. Jerry Randell was feeling pretty much the same way. There was just one bit difference; he and Lita didn't sniff around Joe's Place — they went in for a snifter! They got to the bar and parked posteriors on red-leather stools. They got drinks and Jerry glanced around sourly. The usual collection of punks lounged around the joint. They were guys with vices, shady pasts and uncertain futures, weak guys and vicious guys. At the moment they were polishing the seats with their pants in Joe's Place, their only common bond. Two garish floosies relaxed at a table, obviously resigned to the fact that there wasn't any loose mazuma in the barroom at the moment.

'Some people!' muttered Lita, who didn't usually mix with such flotsam and jetsam. 'Maybe I'd be safer at Erlichs!'

She looked reflective. 'Tommy Berg has an apartment — he liked to hint I should go along with him to it!'

'Well, what's the address, baby?' Jerry asked urgently.

'I — I don't remember! I never went to his lousy apartment — a damn good thing, I think, in the circumstances!'

'But, sugar, try to remember! It might be a lead!'

She stared ahead blankly. After a minute she said: 'I don't remember any address — sorry!'

Jerry Randell got up. 'Could be a lead,' he muttered. 'Get to his apartment and we're gettin' nearer to that snake!'

Jerry walked across the barroom. He sat down slowly beside three sour-looking guys staring over Milwaukee ales. He leaned forward; said in a confiding low voice: 'You guys know Tommy Berg?'

Only one moved his head. The other

two continued to look like they'd been drinking watered dung. 'Yeah.'

'Know his address?' muttered Jerry.

'Why ya ask, bud?'

'I wanna see him — that's why. Gotta proposition for him. What's his address?'

'A room over on Adams Street,' said the other sourly. '213 Adams Street, I guess. That's where he was livin' last.'

'Thanks, pal,' said Jerry curtly, and he slid away and came back to Lita.

'There's always somebody in a barroom who knows something about somebody else,' he said. 'I got his crummy address. Let's go.'

'Tommy Berg?' she asked. 'I've been wondering what all this is to me, but I'd like to see you give that guy hell for the way he treated my anatomy.'

'I whipped him up at Tujunga,' said Jerry. 'But I'll do it again if it'll make you happy.'

His auto was in the small parking lot outside Joe's Place. They slid into it.

The trip to Adams Street was only minutes of tooling through concrete-lined streets lined with other big mechanical slugs, Adams Street wasn't in the lettuce. It was a dreary corridor of crummy apartment houses inhabited by folks who apparently thought the hell with the wonderful vision of an America packed from coast to coast with stucco bungalows, washing machines, refrigerators, television and air-conditioning!

Jerry Randell stopped the car just after he had passed number 213 and then he stared back at the building.

'So that's how you slick guys live,' he said. 'In lowdown joints!' He drummed his fingers on the steering wheel. 'Well, I don't expect to find Tommy Berg up in that apartment whaling hell out of Hairyface because he won't and can't talk! But maybe there's a lead somewhere.'

He got out of the auto. 'You stick here, sugar. I'm gonna snoop.'

She didn't offer any objection and he walked away. He went into the open hall of the building; stared briefly at the grubby row of cards. Tommy Berg's name wasn't even on show. As a starter, Jerry went up the stairs with firm, deliberate steps.

On the second landing he found Tommy Berg's door. He listened outside; there was no sound. He tried the handle; the door was locked. All the signs looked like the guy wasn't at home — as Jerry had known was most likely. Tommy Berg would be someplace convenient for extracting information from an unwilling guy. And Cal Owen and Rick Egler would be closer to him than his own sweat!

So far everything was a bum lead.

Jerry Randell was holding the door handle when another door on the landing opened and a woman stationed herself in the opening and stared insolently at him. She idly fluffed up her garish blonde hair with a hand that had blood-red nails. She smiled with her eyes.

'Seems like the guy ain't in,' she observed. 'You wanna leave a message?'

Jerry Randell looked at her and shook his head. 'I don't want to leave a message,' he said. 'Just figured to find him in.'

'That so-and-so,' she sneered. 'You figured to find that guy in! He only sleeps here an' that ain't every night.'

'Okay,' Jerry drawled. 'Forget I called. I'll see Tommy Berg someplace else.'

'You gotta name? I could tell him you called.'

Jerry grinned. 'Just skip it, sister.'

The grin dropped out of her eyes and a hard, sour look snapped in.

She cursed him silently and banged the door shut in his face. He turned, grinning. His nostrils dilated as he evaded the waft of stale scent the moving door had shot out.

Jerry Randell got to the next landing. He was turning swiftly around the central pillar of the balustrade when he cannoned into a man. In effect, they rammed into each other. Jerry was plenty surprised, although it did not halt his reaction. The other man wasn't surprised at all because he had been mounting the stairs with a heater in his fist.

The man was Tommy Berg, no less!

The gun in his hand made a vicious hack at Jerry Randell's head within a split second of the meeting, proving that Tommy Berg had expected to slam up against the guy who was now his enemy.

Jerry got an anguished glimpse of the slashing weapon and he jerked desperately. The gun scraped down the side of his face and thudded onto his shoulder. Luckily there was some padding in his jacket. It took the steam out of the thump but the side of his face stung like a burn.

Jerry Randell's fists swung only a second after the gun butt brought a grimace to his face. He rammed a right and left at Tommy Berg's head; felt his bunched knuckles grate satisfyingly on flesh and bone. Tommy Berg staggered back, his own first move completed but not effective. Jerry went at the man, determined not to let up. Instinctively, he wanted the guy's gun out of the way.

The two men mixed it for the space of about a minute, neither getting the edge on the other. Tommy Berg did not drop his gun. He didn't use it either, principally because Jerry did not give him much chance.

Sudden running feet on the stairs indicated the approach of someone in a hurry, and it sounded like a man.

It was!

9

Lita Rossini sat in Jerry Randell's auto and gave a scared glance at the man beside her. He held a gun close to her hip, low down so that a chance passer-by should not see it. Lita had last seen this blue-shave chin, rat-trap mouth and bulbous nose when she and Jerry Randell had first been jumped about the missing map. Well, there wasn't a map any more — just a lunkhead who knew the position of the valuable dope — but Cal Owen was very definitely in the play.

So was Rick Egler. He had just departed, moving rather casually in the wake of Tommy Berg. Rick Egler — the slight wiry hood in a cheap red suit! The two men had dived into the crummy apartment house.

Lita was scared — for herself and for Jerry Randell. The setup was lousy — one of those ironic tricks that Fate hands out like a slap in the face. No sooner had

118

Jerry disappeared into the apartment building than an auto had appeared containing the three hoods, and Tommy Berg had recognised Lita sitting inside Jerry's auto. They'd been over before she'd a chance to gasp!

She didn't know why the three lugs should appear in Adams Street. Their appearance was dangerously real, she did know that. Tommy Berg, especially, hated Jerry.

Cal Owen was the pawing type of guy. His mouth held a leer; his eyes a nasty grin. She shot her hand down; gripped his wrist and essayed her strength against his.

'Just keep still!' he snarled. 'Ya wouldn't like me to blow a hole in them hips, would ya? You an' that interferin' shamus! Aw, so what the hell — we'll soon grab that dope only I guess Tommy Berg wants to even with that two-cent dick.'

'You dirt!' snapped Lita. 'Keep your hands off me!'

There was a certain amount of struggle. She got a hint that his gun was bluff. He wasn't going to shoot and attract attention. She wasn't that important. He was just using his heater to keep her quiet.

'Sit still, sister!' snarled Cal Owen. 'Tommy Berg and Rick will deal with the shamus.'

She didn't like sitting next to a louse and she didn't like the idea of Jerry Randell being dealt with! All at once she struck furiously, disregarding the gun. Her fists banged angrily against his bulbous nose and brought out a yell of pain and rage. She shot a hand to the door handle; got it open a bit. He grabbed her arm and held her back. She kicked and felt her shoe crack satisfactorily against his shin. But he still held her. He wasn't using the gun. Her guess about that had been correct. With the prospects of valuable dope for sale in the near future, Cal Owen wasn't starting the racket of gunplay over a girl who was no use to him.

Lita Rossini rapped viciously at the grim wrist holding her. The car door was slightly open. If only she could get away — that was her only thought.

Cal Owen got sick of fighting with a girl. He raised his hand and thudded the open palm heavily against her temple.

Lita felt the dazed nausea flood through her immediately. Another unpleasant blow hit her soggily. She thought she was falling endlessly.

Actually, her body slumped back against the seat and her head sank. With her eyes shut, she was temporarily out of this world. Cal Owen's cunning blows had seen to that.

Cursing, he wondered when the hell the other two would return! Did they figure to bust the guy up in the apartment house or bring him out to the auto so that he could be cut to hell later? Coming to the apartment house had been a queer turn of events. Tommy Berg had wanted a cute set of torture knuckle-dusters to use on the lunkhead. They hadn't expected to run into Jerry Randell and the girl. It didn't make any flaming difference. Tommy Berg had been happy about the setup.

Cal Owen got sudden answers to his ruminations. Men appeared on the doorstep of the crummy apartment joint. Two men were carrying a third. The two guys, Cal was pleased to observe, were Tommy Berg and Rick Egler and they were healthy enough to heave an unconscious gink between them!

Lita Rossini was still dazed but she was stirring when Tommy Berg and Rick Egler hauled Jerry up to an auto that lay behind Jerry Randell's car. The shamus was bundled into the second auto. Blood was streaming from a gash on one side of his head.

'Okay, sister, this is where you transfer,' grunted Cal Owen and, taking advantage of the girl's dazed state, he hauled her out of Jerry's auto and carried her to the other car. All this in seconds and no one walked up in Adams Street to inquire what the hell was cooking. Adams Street was the kind where most folks kept their noses out of other people's businesses. Even in daylight the three thugs were able to get away with their moves.

The auto suddenly moved off with a whining engine. Jerry's car was left at the curb. Cal Owen was driving and Rick

Egler sat beside him but with his wiry little body turned so that he could keep tabs on what was doing in the back. Tommy Berg sat close to Jerry, a gun tickling the dick's ribs. Rick Egler was in a position to waggle his heater in front of Lita's eyes. As the auto moved, she stared around her, the whole hateful position well aware to her mind.

'Some haul!' gloated Tommy Berg. 'I turn up for my knuckle-dusters and run into this — the dame I'd like to make and a guy I'd like to kill, but slowly!'

'You're dirt!' she spat at him.

'Baby, you'd better quit talkin' like that! I don't like it! I don't like the idea of Randell whippin' me up in that goddam wood! Nobody treats me like that and gets away with it! And you, sugar — you've given me the brush-off too many times. I figure to tame you!'

'You're a louse!' slurred a voice. It was Jerry Randell speaking. His awakening wits had rushed him back into this bit of unpleasantness. 'Stop this heap and let Lita get out. She isn't really in this hell-around.'

'Be your age,' sneered Tommy Berg. 'She'd call the cops fast as those high-heels hit the sidewalk!'

'Why should you worry? She doesn't know where you're going. Let her go.'

'Aw, shaddup! You think I'm wet? She'd yell for cops, sure thing. The cops are interested in dope. Relax, Randell — you ain't got long to live!'

The auto was rolling steadily through the cement jungle that was Los Angeles. Traffic tooled swiftly on all sides through the straight wide street. They passed cops aplenty but ignorance is bliss and one half of the world doesn't know what the other half is doing!

'Where you got Hairyface?' snapped Jerry Randell. He put a handkerchief to his head; brought it away and looked at the blood.

'That creep? You call him Hairyface?' Tommy Berg was sneeringly amused. 'Well, it fits. Don't worry about him. Worry about yourself, swine! I'm gonna fix ya for beatin' me up in that wood.' His voice thickened. 'I hate your goddam guts for that, Randell!'

'You're bein' juvenile!' sneered Jerry. 'I've told you to let Lita go free. She won't call the cops. She is scared of the whole setup. That right, Lita? Say you'll — '

'Aw, can it!' snarled Tommy Berg. 'You two are comin' with us.'

'Why not take 'em for a ride?' suggested Rick Egler, staring from the front seat. 'We don't need these two birds.'

'I got things to settle.'

'Rick's right,' came Cal Owen's voice. He did not turn his head; he was concentrating on driving. 'All we want is make that lunkhead show us where the dope is hidden. We don't need these two fools. Let's get rid of them fast.'

'We can handle everythin'!' raged Tommy Berg. 'I put you two guys onto gettin' this dope. So I figure to have my say. I'm gonna fix this lousy shamus and I'm gonna make this dame wish I was her pal.'

'You fools!' shrieked Lita. 'Hairyface shifted the dope. He moved it to another place! He's the only one who knows where to find the stuff!'

The auto nearly jolted. But Cal Owen wasn't too much startled. Jerry Randell hissed: 'Shaddup!' But Lita was slightly crazed and repeated:

'Hairyface shifted the dope! We couldn't find it!'

'So that's the angle,' grated Tommy Berg. 'So only that gink knows the whereabouts of the dope!'

'That doesn't matter,' observed Rick Egler. 'He'll be glad to show us the hideout.'

'You can wager on that,' gritted Tommy Berg. 'And we aim to get that lousy dope today!'

Cal Owen's expert driving took the auto from one crummy downtown area to another. The car went slowly through some narrow streets of L.A. Chinatown. Jerry Randell guessed the driver was reaching his destination. Finally the car nosed into an alley.

Jerry stared bitterly at the gun Tommy Berg poked into his ribs.

'Don't try any superman tricks,' sneered Tommy Berg. 'I'll plug you dead before

I'll let you trick me. And I ain't bluffin'.'

The auto stopped. It was a moment of tension. Jerry Randell could have tried to beat a slug — only he had never heard of the man who had done that and lived. Lita Rossini was looking scared again. She wasn't a crook or a dick and didn't like this rumpus. There was no knowing what Lita might do. Jerry watched her intently and hoped she wouldn't start anything crazy.

★ ★ ★

Jerry glanced out of the nearest window and saw the grimy brickwork of old five-storey buildings. He was staring at the backs of these premises and thinking it was just like these lugs to have a hideout in Chinatown. The Chinese community were not to blame for the scum that floated with them. All communities have scum.

The gun jabbed wickedly into him again. 'Oke. We're movin'. If ya want a fast ticket to hell now; just play it tricky!'

Tommy Berg's hand whipped smoothly

127

up and fingers plucked at the heater in Jerry's armpit holster. Jerry started forward a bit and slowed with a bitter grin. The other's gun was still the deciding factor.

'We're gettin' out!'

But Jerry Randell's feet no sooner touched the ground than the alley became the scene for fast, brutal play. While Tommy Berg held his heater like a cannon, Cal Owen swung a sly gun butt against Jerry's head. It was a deft tap, nicely applied by a man who had had the experience in these things. Jerry swayed, darkness flooding into his brain. As he sagged, the thugs held him. Tommy Berg grabbed at Lita Rossini and cut off her screams with a big hand over her mouth. In this way, after only seconds of the rough stuff, Jerry and the girl were hustled from the auto and into the grimy five-storey building. A door in a high wall swung behind them and the alley was silent again.

Jerry Randell was out to the world for only minutes but he didn't know that. It seemed a terribly long time when he painfully opened his eyes again. He grimaced as his head hurt. There was the usual feeling of nausea alter a rough house. His mind worked swiftly because this wasn't the first time he'd taken a wallop on the head. First thing he discovered were the bindings on his wrists and ankles.

He stared around and saw the setting was a lousy cellar. The trip in the auto and the dirty play in the alley flooded back into his mind. He glanced around and saw Lita Rossini lying on a bed. Only her hands were tied for she threshed her beautiful legs.

And that was not so good, for Tommy Berg and Cal Owen and Rick Egler were looking on.

There was a third man in no less grim circumstances. Jerry stared at Hairyface and thought his bruised face told enough. He was tied to a wooden chair and his chin sagged down on his chest. In front of him was a dirty table and a sheet of paper and a pencil. The paper was messed up with blood. It was creased and crumpled, too.

The three thugs were enjoying a quiet smoke, evidently waiting for Hairyface to return to this world. As Jerry moved on the floor, Tommy Berg shot him a sneering glance,

'So the shamus is comin' outa it! Say, maybe I oughta start some fun now! Maybe this is where I oughta knock hell outa you for the way you treated me up in the wood!'

'Let's concentrate on this lunkhead!' growled Cal Owen immediately, and he just about ate his cigarette. 'This is the guy who'll show a percentage. It's that damned dope we want, remember!'

'Okay,' steered Tommy Berg, 'we concentrate on the lunkhead — get him to make the drawing of where he's hidden the goddamn dope seein' he can't talk!' He swung to Jerry mockingly. 'That's a break for you, pally — but don't count on it lastin'!'

Just to emphasise the fact, he got off his seat and came to Jerry Randell. His first act was to kick the shamus in the ribs; his next was to bend low and swing a nasty punch into Jerry's jaw. Then he returned to the table and calmly lit another Camel.

Jerry Randell spat out and moved his jaw. The knifing pain subsided. Wind returned to his lungs and his ribs quit creaking. He sat and hated the slick louse who had done it.

Tommy Berg grabbed at Hairyface's shoulder and shook him. Cal Owen picked up a jug and sloshed water over their captive's hirsute face.

Hairyface's wild eyes glared at his captors. He began to shake his head in refusal. Tommy Berg slowly untied the man's right arm.

'Start drawing, feller. I figure you're not as crazy as you look and I reckon you can make a drawin'. Don't try to be tricky. You'd stick here until we located the dope, so don't try to trick us with a phoney drawing. I wish I'd had time to get my knuckle-dusters outa my apartment but that play was bust to hell. Okay, you got some goddam paper and a pencil — start making a map. You know where you hid that dope. Make a start or by hell you'll get some more treatment!'

Rick Egler threw down his cigarette

butt, and stamped on it. 'Say, let's take this lunkhead up to Tujunga Lake an' make him show us the goddam place instead of havin' a blasted map.'

Cal Owen shot a wary glance at Tommy Berg.

'Yeah, how about that? Seems faster.'

Tommy Berg looked sour. 'Yeah? And have the rube escape from us? Or maybe attract a cop!'

'I don't see how he'll do that,' snarled Cal Owen, and his blue-shave chin jutted angrily. 'I figure all this foolin' around is a waste o' time! I said so from the start! I still say it!'

'Yeah, that's the way I feel,' supported Rick Egler. 'Let's hell up to the lake again an' get this fool to show us the dope cache.'

'All right, if that's the way you guys want to play it,' said Tommy Berg sullenly. 'We'll go up — now.'

'Swell. We want that dope today. Let's waste no more time.'

Jerry Randell listened to the altercation with narrowed eyes and a feeling of relief. Maybe this was the break; at least it didn't give Tommy Berg time to taste his vengeance. With Cal Owen and Rick Egler pressing him. he'd have to postpone his potential sadistic tête-à-tête.

The three men were engaged for the next few minutes in untying Hairyface from the chair and then binding his hands together behind his back. This was done despite his struggles. The bearded man made moaning, furious sounds. In a way, Jerry Randell was sorry for the lunkhead. It was a sure bet that curtains lay ahead for the guy as soon as the three thugs located the dope. But maybe behind his barrier of speechlessness Hairyface wasn't so dumb and knew that!

Then the party was ready to move out of the cellar. Cal Owen shot a disgruntled glance at Jerry Randell and Lita.

'These two birds are gonna be a lousy nuisance. I figure we oughta just leave 'em here until we get that dope shifted to where we want it. After that, the hell with these two. I don't see why I should stick my neck out on a murder rap making corpses outa these two!'

'Leave them to me,' snarled Tommy Berg.

Rick Egler grunted in support of his pal. 'Sure thing. This part is your idea an' you're stuck with it! Me — I think like Cal. We oughta get that dope moved to someplace safe. Hell, that's the only thing that interests me! There ain't no percentage on these two!'

'I got ideas for them!' raged Tommy Berg. 'This two-bit dick knocked me around! And the dame always gave me the brushoff. Let me tell you guys if Randell was in circulation he'd ball up any attempt to get that dope — you oughta know that.'

'Okay.' Cal Owen hung on to Hairyface as if he was old man mountain. 'Okay! Just let's get this palooka up to the lakeside an' locate that dope. Play about with these two some other time! Jeeze, help me with this goon, will ya?'

The three men hauled the struggling Hairyface out of the cellar, taking him, presumably, to the auto. Jerry Randell watched them disappear and then he began to struggle mightily against his bonds, He'd been tied with lightweight manila rope and it was good enough to hold anybody but an escapist for hours. He shouted over to Lita:

'Can you come over? Your legs ain't tied, baby. Maybe you could slacken the rope around my wrists! Quick! Those punks won't be gone more'n a minute.'

She slid off the small, odorous bed and got close to him. She turned her back to him and he rolled over so that she could get her fingers on to the ropes around his wrists. He knew damned well it was only a slight chance but he'd be a fool not to take the slimmest opportunity to turn the tables for Tommy Berg wasn't kidding when he ranted on about hating somebody's guts! This, in fact, was a fight for life! It wasn't something off a TV serial!

Lita's varnished fingernails plucked at the ropes with grim determination. She knew Tommy Berg was a sadist at heart and was apparently storing up some lousy tricks to use on her. She didn't want her body to be the chopping-block!

Suddenly she darted away from Jerry Randell. It was a break for them that her legs were not tied. She knew there were only minutes of freedom. She moved quickly to a locker set beside the smelly bed, turned and slid a drawer open. Her fingers fumbled inside the drawer and drew out a fairly sharp knife. It was only a second's work to push the drawer shut and move swiftly to Jerry again. Without words, he twisted until his bound wrists were in a position for her to start operation saw.

In the tension of the moment she hacked the blade awkwardly against his bindings and heard him give a sharp inward hiss.

'Did I cut you?'

'Get on with it!' he breathed. 'Those slobs will be back any minute. If they come, drop the knife behind me and take a run for the bed. We've got to fool them, baby!'

He had a hunch the men would return before Lita could successfully cut through his ropes. There came the sound of voices and feet. It sounded like two of them were coming back. Lita dropped the knife and jumped for the bed.

10

Tommy Berg and Cal Owen entered the cellar again and immediately the former picked up a length of rope and advanced to the girl. 'Mustn't forget about you, baby!' he leered.

He looped rope around her ankles and tied it like she was some animal destined for the slaughterhouse He sneered down at her when it was done then crudely slapped her on her behind.

'Relax, sugar. I'll be back. For some fun, huh?' He inclined his head to Jerry Randell. 'And hell for the two-bit dick. I'll teach him to beat me up!' Again the vicious streak in his voice showed his real hatred of the private eye.

Jerry lay still and glowered. All he wanted was the two lugs out of the cellar. Sure they could bolt the door — he'd tackle that later.

Lita glared at Tommy Berg couldn't resist having what she thought might be the last word.

'You're a louse, Tommy,' she snapped. 'I never knew you were so goddam low. You could get under a snake's belly!'

'Aw, shaddup!' He slammed his palm against her cheek. He stared down as the red flush rushed into her face. He wet his lips with his tongue. 'I got some cute ideas for you, sugar. But right now we ain't got time.'

Cal Owen's rat-trap mouth worked. 'Say, let's move it. These two are okay. This cellar is soundproof an' old Chang don't give a damn.'

Even so, Tommy Berg itched for some satisfaction and got it by kicking savagely at Jerry as he passed on the way to the door. The kick swung painfully into Jerry's thigh, jolting him around and painting a grimace on his face.

Cal Owen lightly grabbed Tommy Berg's sleeve and they went out of the cellar. There was the sound of the door being locked. Jerry stared grimly at the barred window and the dirty glass. No way out there — but he wasn't worrying about that.

He waited until he was sure the three

lugs were in the auto with the hapless Hairyface. There was no sound of a departing car. The cellar was pretty soundproof.

Then he strained grimly at his bonds around his wrists. He was pretty sure the rope was cut almost through at one part. His bunched hands were sticky with blood. Lita had done a nice job of butchering!

The rope gave almost at once. He wrenched away with grim satisfaction and felt his hands slide out of the bonds. Free! He twisted and grabbed at the knife. Lita gave an exclamation of pleasure and he found time to grin at her. Then he leaned forward and hacked through the rope around his legs. After that it was the work of only a moment to jump right over to the girl and cut her free.

She slid off the bed, put her arms around Jerry and kissed him impulsively.

As they parted, she lifted his hand and her green eyes widened at the sight of the blood.

'I'll have to bandage that!'

'Forget it. Let's move it.'

'No. You want blood poisoning or something?'

She lifted her dress and Jerry heard a tearing sound. It lasted a few seconds and then the dress hemline swished back like a delightful curtain. Lita Rossini had a length of silky material,

'Put your hand up,' she commanded.

'You don't have to do this. Why should you tear bits out of your damned pretties?'

'I want to. I guess we can get out of here now. You've saved me from something pretty lousy, big boy.'

She tied the material around his wrist and it did stop the bleeding. He grinned and dropped his arm.

'Okay. Let's get to hell out of here!'

An examination of the door showed that it was bolted on the other side with a couple of bolts. Jerry went to the window and inspected the bars. He decided the door would have to be forced.

There was another door inside the cellar-room that he figured would lead to other parts of the building. He remembered Cal Owen saying something about

'Chang'. Seemed that was the Chinaman who owned the house. The other door, which was locked, would give access into the old house but Jerry Randell didn't want to get into the damned house — he wanted to be out of it! And he wasn't interested in any tussles with the Chinese underworld!

There was only one way to get out and that was by smashing down the door. He hoped the bolt socket would give way under his weight. And he hoped he could do the trick quickly because the noise might easily bring someone to the cellar.

There wasn't anything in the room to use as a hammer so it had to he his own weight. He made the first thud against the door, gritting his teeth as his whole frame jarred unpleasantly. It sure wasn't any goddam door on a movie set! It wasn't made of balsa wood and it certainly didn't bust open with an impressive show of splinters!

Jerry Randell just about shook the guts out of himself over the door and he got his grim satisfaction as, bit by bit, he felt, something giving. It was the woodwork, he thought. He hammered away, bunched shoulders ramming into the thick door. He heard something crack agonisingly and he thudded again. Something snapped — metal or something shearing off — maybe a screw. He ran at the door again, a human battering-ram. It was a hefty door and not like some of the plywood affairs they were building into the little stucco bungalows out by the San Fernando valley.

Lita Rossini waited in unbearable excitement. She kept glancing at the other door, expecting someone to interrupt the breakout. But no one came. Finally Jerry had the door groggy; the bolt sockets were giving up. A last thud and the door shattered outwards, the hinges twisted and protesting.

'Let's move.' Jerry rubbed his right shoulder. 'Let's get after those guys!'

Lita nearly choked. 'Gee! You don't mean you're going to hell after those three lugs again?'

He grabbed her arm. 'C'mon, let's get out! If you figure to start arguin', do it somewhere in the street.'

With that he hustled her through a

courtyard to a door that opened at a turn of a knob. In seconds they were in the alley and he quickly escorted her to the nearest street.

They were a dishevelled pair who hailed a cab some moments later and the driver was entitled to give them a curious stare. But they got into the cab.

'First I want another heater,' explained Jerry to Lita. 'And then I want to pick up my auto. I guess it's still in Adams Street — I hope!'

'And then you hell after those thugs!' she said sarcastically. 'That's great! That's fine! Why should you go after those guys?'

'That cursed dope, baby! I'm bein' paid to locate that dope and destroy it. Apart from that I've got a score to settle with Tommy Berg.'

'Aw, gee, I should have gone to Erlichs today!' groaned Lita.

'You're goin' to your apartment on Culver Boulevard, anyway,' he said firmly.

'You bet I am. This tear-around is tough on clothes!'

'I meant you'll be safer there.'

'Brother, I don't feel safe anywhere!'

He grinned. 'With that classy chassis, you won't ever be safe anywhere, baby!'

The cab was speeding through the wide city streets of down town Los Angeles. The driver passed the monstrous Telephone Exchange building, took to the huge freeway — that big span of concrete which shoots over the rooftops of a mile of minor streets. Pretty soon the cab was in Slausen Street. It halted while Jerry rushed into his office. He came out some minutes later. He had made a lightning change and was now in a fawn tropical worsted suit. He also wore another heater in his shoulder rig. The silky bandage still decorated his wrist, however. He wore it like a badge.

He got into the cab and sat close to Lita — maybe a bit too close, for a sarky smile quirked the cabby's lips when he glanced in the rear view mirror.

It needed only a few minutes more and they hit Adams Street and there Jerry paid off the cabby. His own auto was still at the kerb and he and Lita transferred to it.

'Okay, you go home, baby,' he muttered.

He drove her to Culver Boulevard and stopped the car. He turned and gave her a swift kiss.

'Okay, baby, you go to your apartment an' stick there an' change your clothes. I'll be seein' you — '

'You're going to hell after those guys — ' she choked. 'Look, feller, you could slick the police onto this! I'd like you to come back to me — and I don't mean in a meat wagon! You'll hit grief chasing those thugs, I — '

'Now look,' he interrupted, 'don't worry about a thing. And I haven't time to waste. Relax in your apartment, kid, and get some sleep. Keep yourself full of pep for my return.'

'And you keep healthy,' she retorted. 'Cadavers can't kiss!'

'We're wastin' time,' he muttered. 'I got to hit the trail. Those slobs will be snoopin' around Tujunga by now. There's only one thing — I figure Hairyface is a pretty obstinate guy! I'm bankin' on that.'

Impulsively, she wasted more of his time by kissing him. He slid her arms off his neck.

'Got to get goin', sugar.'

She got out of the auto and crossed over the sidewalk to the accompaniment of a rapid tattoo of heels. Then Jerry Randell shot the car away from the kerb. He moved fast down Culver and stopped at the first fill-up station. He figured he was low on gas, and he didn't want to run out somewhere up near Tujunga Lake.

After that, he was tooling the car out of the built-up areas of L.A. He thought it was queer that the scene should jerk back to Tujunga Lake again. But the dope was up there and grim men after it.

In her apartment, Lita Rossini stared around and thought a terrible lot had happened since that morning. Was it just that morning she had awakened to find Jerry Randell in the bed beside her? It seemed like a million years ago! Too much had happened. The hell-around had moved with incredible speed, sweeping her into violent conflicts with ruthless men. She wasn't accustomed to violence.

She lit a cigarette and smoked it fast while her thoughts ranged far and wide. She realised she was badly worried about

Jerry Randell tearing up to Tujunga to tangle with gunnies and thugs. The lug might get himself killed! She choked over her smoke.

There was only one thing to do — she saw it with sudden clarity. She'd phone the police and have them all over the lakeside in no time. They would stop any gunplay between Jerry and the three thugs and maybe they would locate the hidden dope and so bring the lousy run-around to a close. Certainly the cops were interested in the dope. They wouldn't want it distributed to underground pedlars. A squad of police all over Tujunga Lake would certainly make a clean-up. Jerry might be mad, seeing he considered himself hired to do the job, but at least he'd be healthy!

Lita thought that Lieutenant Strang would be interested in knowing the dope was hidden somewhere around Tujunga Lake. Yes, he was the guy she'd contact.

Her hand went to the phone and she began dialling.

In the meantime, Jerry Randell was pushing along the highway, his foot feeding gas to the engine. He did not expect to really catch up with the three thugs because they had had a good head start, but he'd get to the scene in nice time to bust up their play — he hoped. That dope wasn't going to leave the lakeside. He was determined about that! He wasn't a whitewashed moralist but he knew the social damage the consignment of dope could cause among some crazy dope-takers of Los Angeles. The vice had even contaminated teenage kids who figured it was smart to buy the stuff from lousy little pedlars frequenting third-rate cafés.

He didn't know how he'd bust up the play of the three thugs; he guessed it might work out. He had a heater. He wanted to get Hairyface out of the hands of those men; somehow he felt sorry for the big dumb guy.

The fifteen miles were covered quickly and he drove up the dirt road. It was like paying a return visit to an old familiar scene. He knew the dirt road could lead him right into grief. But at least he wouldn't be expected. Tommy Berg and his pals figured him for a trussed-up dick in the cellar!

Jerry knew this was an advantage and he tooled the heap into a leafy nook and left it, proceeding on foot. He'd have to Injun up to the cabin and the surrounding locale. When he jumped the other men, he'd get a notion of how to tackle them. But what he really wanted was to destroy the cached dope. After that was accomplished, the three thugs could go to hell — unless they insisted on mixing it!

The leafy background was silent except for the rustle of gently-waving branches and the twitter of a few birds. Of other vacationers there was no sight. The sun lay heavy and hot on the land. He saw the cabin ahead, standing with a deserted appearance. He waited a moment and decided the three men were some way off. There wasn't even any sign of their auto. Probably they had it parked out of sight behind some leafy cover. And Hairyface was undoubtedly with his captors. The man was suffering from a flesh-wound in addition to the rough treatment he'd get from the three thugs. Altogether not a good time for the hapless stooge.

Jerry Randell moved carefully across the clearing and reached the side of the cabin. He listened for a moment with his ear pressed to the wood wall. He decided there wasn't anyone inside the cabin. Empty. He darted away and made for the nearest clump of bushes. He didn't like moving around in the open — not when there were three enemies in the vicinity.

Jerry immediately discovered the parked auto belonging to the three thugs. It lay behind a leafy screen and was ready for driving out. He walked around it and grinned thinly. Maybe Tommy Berg thought he would drive away from this spot with a valuable consignment of dope!

Jerry lifted the hood. He gave a brief glance at the electrical layout. He thought he could fix this car so that it would not start.

At that moment a fiendish scream shot through the air. The sound came from the thick clump of trees and bushes that lay right down to the lake's edge. The sound had been an animalistic mixture of snarl and scream of pain. Jerry knew just what it meant.

Hairyface was having the rough treatment!

Jerry Randell jumped away from the auto and the hood fell down with a metallic crash. With all thoughts and faculties bent on the unnerving sound that had rent the air, he forgot all about immobilising the auto.

He raced away and then, as he got into the thick greenery, he slowed cautiously. But his shoes picked a fast way between bushes and his body shouldered through clinging branches. His gun was out of the shoulder rig and decorated his right fist.

He heard the sounds of a sudden fight ahead. There was the harsh rustling as men pressed against bushes and the crackling sound of breaking twigs and branches. Jerry heard grunts as men fought and then a sobbing, inhuman yell that he knew could come only from Hairyface.

Feeling sick of this brutality, Jerry pressed on. He parted a thick bush and then found himself staring at a lousy scene.

Hairyface, his hands still tied behind his back, was fighting like a crazed animal. Tommy Berg, Cal Owen and Rick Egler were holding him and at the same time propelling him towards an old timber jetty that stuck out from the lakeside. Near to the jetty was the remains of an old ruined boathouse. Jerry took the scene in with a fast glance.

Hairyface was fighting like an enraged brute but his hands being behind his back had him handicapped. The three thugs got the big man onto the rotten old jetty even as Jerry Randell, startled into slow reaction, stared. In another few seconds Hairyface was pushed and heaved at the edge of the jetty. The black lake water swirled lazily. Jerry realized in a fleeting flash of thought that it wasn't really very deep at this point but deep enough to drown a man — especially a man with his hands tied behind his back!

11

Jerry Randell raised his heater and snapped off an angry shot that buzzed close to the three men who were thrusting Hairyface to the edge of the jetty. His anger affected his aim and the slug missed Cal Owen by an inch. The gunshot really startled the three thugs and two things happened. First, Rick Egler whipped out a heater and flashed a fast shot in Jerry's direction. This was another furious shot and missed its target. Secondly, Hairyface was given the final push and he fell backwards into the lake. There was a loud splash, a smothered yell and the water closed over him.

It doesn't take long to drown a man. Jerry got that in a flash. He also knew a slug can spell finis even faster than drowning! He jumped back into the cover of the screening bushes as three guns sang a fast, gleeful tune and slugs spat all around him. He also went down fast as a spooked animal.

But he had a direction and he wasn't running away from the three lice with the guns. He actually plunged through the tangle of undergrowth in the direction of the lakeside. The tangled bushes grew right down to the water's edge. The ruined boathouse and jetty stood in a small clearing that was probably smaller than it had ever been owing to the encroaching undergrowth. He could get to the lake's edge and still be in the cover of the bushes. No doubt the greenery would not stop a slug, but at least it hindered accurate shooting.

He was grimly counting the seconds during his scramble like an animal through the undergrowth. No more shots came his way. Seemed like the three gunnies didn't want too much noise of heaters. Jerry was counting the seconds because he was wondering if Hairyface could swim with his hands tied behind his back. Maybe he couldn't swim at all. If so, he was in a helluva spot.

In another few seconds of frantic movement through the undergrowth,

Jerry saw the black water ahead. He also heard confused shouts behind him and guessed the thugs were yelling contradictory orders at each other. He didn't stop to think about them. He poised at the lakeside and whipped off his jacket. Then he slipped off his shoulder rig, stuffed the gun into the holster and, wrapping it in the coat, stowed it under a bush. Marking the bush with a glance, he waded quickly into the lake.

The water soon got deep, surprisingly so. He swam fast, using the powerful crawl. He was near to the rotten old jetty very quickly. The lakeshore was not far away and presumably the three gunnies, but he didn't give them a thought. He was searching for Hairyface.

He spotted the body threshing wildly about five yards beyond the edge of the jetty. Then, as it sank again, he struck out for the man. He guessed he was no swimmer and was probably drowning. Jerry wondered why he wanted to rescue the lunkhead and he didn't know the answer. Could be he was just sorry for him. Anyway, he was a human being and drowning like a tied mongrel was a lousy way to go out.

The swim wasn't difficult but his troubles started the moment he grabbed the man. Hairyface was crazed with fear and he writhed like some obscene specimen sinking unwillingly into hell. The fact that the man's hands were tied was some advantage to Jerry Randell. It stopped him from clawing and wrestling. But Hairyface kicked crazily. Jerry grabbed the man's shoulders and began the haul back. He did it in spite of the man's kicking and writhing. Jerry made for the part of the lakeshore where he had left his coat. There was cover from the overhanging bushes there. And there was his gun. Where the hell the three thugs were he had no idea.

When finally he got his half-drowned man to the land, he realised there was a strange silence all around. Jerry listened for about three seconds and did not hear any rustling or shouting — and certainly no gunshots.

It seemed that the three hoodlums had scrammed.

Jerry turned to Hairyface. The man was making some lousy noises and spewing water. He looked like a half-drowned rat. His hairy face had taken a beating and blood welled from cuts and slashes. Jerry pulled grimly at the ropes for some moments and then figured the taut bindings were not to be easily undone. He went to the bush where he had hidden his coat and holster. He got them out and fumbled in a pocket. He had a small pocket-knife that he had grabbed when he had visited his office on Slausen Street. He got busy on Hairyface's bindings. In moments they were cut through and the man was free. But he was in a bad way and his gulping noises indicated he had swallowed half of Tujunga Lake. Jerry ruthlessly rolled the man over on to his belly and gave him some massage treatment.

Hairyface brought back a great amount of the lake and then sat up and groaned and gasped. His eyes flicked sullenly at Jerry frequently. Jerry wrung the water out of his pants and then got into his shoulder rig and jacket again. With the

157

heavy heater under his armpit, he felt better. He looked around and suddenly wondered about the hidden auto belonging to the three lice.

Jerry rose and hauled Hairyface to his feet. The man swayed a bit but seemed to be recovering.

'Did those guys get the dope?' Jerry snapped, and he stared keenly at the bearded face. He cursed inwardly when the man nodded sullenly.

'How?' Jerry swore at his own stupid question when he realised the man's battered face explained that. 'Where was the stuff? Where'd you hide it?'

Hairyface raised an arm and pointed through the bushes. Jerry glanced along the line of direction. Hairyface tugged at his jacket and set off with a shambling stride. Jerry walked behind him; noted the congealed blood on the man's shirt, near the shoulder. He marvelled that the big man could keep going, but maybe the slug wasn't in the wound. It hardly seemed possible. Hairyface wore only a tattered shirt and thick pants. With his inability to speak, he looked pretty primitive.

The man led the way and they pushed through to the small clearing around the jetty and ruined boathouse, and here Hairyface pointed and made queer noises with his gums. He was pointing at the ruined boathouse!

'You put the consignment in there?' exclaimed Jerry.

There was a violent nodding of the man's head.

'And those lugs have got the stuff?'

More nods seemed to signify agreement. Jerry turned grimly. He tapped Hairyface on the arm.

'You follow me for a change, bud,' he snapped.

Jerry Randell led the way through the lakeside greenery and presently they came to the spot where he had seen the parked auto belonging to the thugs.

There was a little difference; the car was gone. Only the tyre marks proved that it had ever been there.

'For hell's sake!' muttered Jerry. 'They got the stuff! After all this goddam foolin' around they got the dope! Looks like the time lag was enough for 'em to beat the truth out of Hairyface and then shift the dope to the auto. And to think I was starin' at the car'. The dope must have been stowed in the luggage boot. Fast loading — but there were three guys to do the work. And then they figured to get rid of Hairyface — and that's where I turned up!' He ended bitterly: 'The too-late shamus! Now that lousy dope is bein' taken someplace else!'

He spun on his heel and at that moment the sound of whining auto engines surged with increasing audibility into the air.

Jerry Randell walked forward, Hairy-face at his heel like a titanic Man Mountain. He reached the cabin belonging to the late unlamented Abe Craster when the first of the cars tore up the dirt trail.

Then it seemed in the next few seconds he was surrounded by cops. There were two cars, big and full of cops. Jerry grinned mirthlessly. Apparently he wasn't the only dick who was too late. And he could guess how the cops had been slicked up to Tujunga Lake. Dear little

Lita Rossini! So the cute little doll had phoned the bulls!

Lieutenant Strang walked up stiffly, his severe blue suit and black hat strange against the rural greenery.

'All right — what's goin' on, Randell? Who's this big guy? Where the hell is that consignment of dope?'

Jerry laughed grimly. 'You got a cigarette? You can turn those cars around right now. Three lugs by the names of Tommy Berg, Rick Egler and Cal Owen lighted out with the dope just five minutes ago. They must have passed you on the highway — I guess you wouldn't have been so dumb as to allow an auto to pass you comin' down the dirt road.'

'We didn't see any auto on the dirt road!' snapped Lieutenant Strang. He swallowed. 'You mean to tell me they got the blasted stuff away from here?'

'That's the setup,' said Jerry. 'Here's the yarn, Strang — you might as well have it. This lug, Hairyface, was Abe Craster's dumb guardian of the cache. Well, he took it from one hiding-place and put it in another. He put it in an old boathouse,'

— Jerry waved a hand — 'just fifty yards from here. Tommy Berg, Rick Egler and Cal Owen got hold of Hairyface an' got the truth out of him. I was just a bit too late. They even had the guy in the lake.'

And Jerry whipped out the rest of the details. There was a detective standing close to Lieutenant Strang and he took down Jerry's account in fast shorthand on a small book. Two other cops walked quickly along to the boathouse just to wise up and look for marks. Strang spent two seconds staring at the spot where the thugs had parked their auto. Another cop made swift drawings of the tyre imprints.

'Okay,' said Strang abruptly. 'Let's go, If we haven't got the dope, we've gotta lead in those three guys' names. Bet they'll have a record. The word will be passed on to the patrol cars to watch for 'em. We'll make 'em for attempting to distribute dope.'

'Nice to hear,' said Jerry.

'Yeah? Why don't you send your client a bill and wind up this investigation, Randell? You like it tough or somethin'?'

'I'm doin' it because I'm crazy,' said

Jerry, and he dragged on the camel one of the cops had given him.

'Yeah? Well, come down to my office when you've cleaned up and sign your statement, will you?'

'Yeah, I'll be pleased to do that for you an' the taxpayers!'

Jerry returned to his own car, which he had parked down the dirt road. Hairyface went with him, shambling along, his head on his chin, an odd grunt issuing from his swollen lips. When they reached the auto, Jerry Randell thought he had hidden it well for the cops had not noticed it! Not that that mattered a hoot in Georgia now.

The dope was being rushed into L.A. That was the one thought that pounded in Jerry's brain. Then another was added: was Lita safe in her apartment right now?

Because it was now obvious to the three thugs that they had escaped from the Chinatown cellar. And with Tommy Berg's in-bitten mind anything could happen.

'Get in beside me!' Jerry snarled to the lunkhead. 'I'm movin' this auto!'

He drove so fast down the dirt lane that

he caught up with the departing cop cars. He couldn't pass on the narrow lane and, in any case, only minutes passed and then the three autos were tearing back to Los Angeles. It was a fast slash back to town on a four-lane highway built for speed. The autos provided it, too.

The pace had to drop considerably when the restricted areas were entered. Even so, Jerry Randell slipped through the wide concrete streets with a good display of driving skill and came to Culver Boulevard, and bounded out of his car as the engine quit. He left Hairyface gaping and ran for the stairs inside the apartment block. He raced up and turned landings until he reached the fourth floor.

Lita's door was open to the turn of the knob. He darted in, a big guy with a taut mouth and grim grey eyes.

Inside the first second he got the fact that Lita was not in the small apartment. Then he noticed the chair lying on its back. There wasn't much more disorder but that was enough. He found her handbag lying behind the chair. It was

164

open and a few of the silly contents spilled out.

He stared for a second and a helluva lot of grim thoughts presented a confused picture in his mind. He was seeing Lita again in that brief second — Lita, the red-head with the defiant greenish eyes.

The second of thought over, he jerked angrily. He didn't need a blueprint. Lita had been hoisted out of her apartment and it had happened not so long ago and the guys responsible were the three thugs.

Jerry paused on that thought. He had a hunch that amended his idea. He figured this was Tommy Berg's gimmick. Cal Owen and Rick Egler were more stuck on getting cash value out of Abe Craster's consignment of dope.

He went out to his auto and the senseless Hairyface.

'Jeeze! Some companion!' he thought bitterly. 'And I ought never to have left that girl! Now they got the dope and Lita! an' what have I got — a lunkhead and a wet shirt!'

He drove quickly and through force of habit back to his office on Slausen. He picked up the phone and dialled the police headquarters. He got Lieutenant Strang's department but he didn't get in touch with that worthy. It didn't matter. Bitterly, he reported how Lita Rossini was missing from her apartment.

Hairyface sat in the office not more than a few minutes. Jerry went up to his room and changed once more and thought the game was hard on his clothes. He donned clean socks, shirt and a pair of old blue worsted trousers. He added a bright necktie and slipped into an old Californian sports coat. He stuck his feet into some old brogues and thought if this outfit got mussed up the hell with it. When he came down to the office again, Hairyface had vanished.

Jerry glanced out of the window into busy Slausen. His car was still at the kerb.

Jerry Randell checked through his gun. He grabbed a hat off a peg — an old one. He felt hungry in spite of his determination to go out into the streets and dig around until he turned a stone that would reveal the whereabouts of a louse called Tommy Berg.

He was at the office door when his phone shrilled again. He turned, his mouth still a firm, taut line. He grabbed the instrument. He figured it would be the cops wanting to know something.

Bit it wasn't.

'You there, Randell?' A chuckle of satisfaction. 'Yeah! I got Lita just where I want her. Quick work, huh?'

Jerry slowly tightened his fingers around the phone until they whitened. 'Let her go, Berg!'

'Sure. Sometime. She's got in my hair, Randell. Like you. I don't forget easy. You — '

'I said let her go, slob!' snarled Jerry, and his hand holding the phone shook with the intensity of his rage. 'Let her go! Let her go!'

'Take it easy, ya nosey shamus! Pity there's only a wire between us — we could take a poke at each other!'

'You got that dope! What do you want with the girl? Let me tell you the cops are lookin' for you! Take her out into the street, Berg, an' put her in a cab before you have more than dope trafficking to answer for. You'll — '

'Sure, we got the dope,' gloated the voice. 'And we're arranging to sell it fast. Damn the cops — they won't get me. I'll leave town — when I'm ready.'

'You're nuts!' taunted Jerry. 'Why should you stick your neck out for a dame? Why give me this call?'

12

'Look, Randell,' sneered Tommy Berg over the line, 'you want to find the dame, huh? Okay, I'll give ya a sporting chance. Me — the great sport! Come on over to the carny ground at Venice Boulevard — know it? A place called Big Tom's Carnival. On the corner of Venice and Pico. Ya know the joint? It won't be alive until about seven. Say ya get there about eight, huh?'

Jerry grated: 'What the hell's this? Where is Lita? I don't get the idea of you as a big sport louse. But I do get that you want me to walk into a cute little trap.'

'You scared of somethin'?' sneered the voice. 'You scared to go find the gal? You're hot-pants for her, ain't ya, Randell? Okay. Take a looksee at Big Tom's Carnival. Who knows — you might find her!'

Jerry Randell's free hand stole to the gun in his holster and then, with a sombre grin that revealed his teeth, he let the heater slide back. He wasn't face to face with Tommy Berg; just talking over a line!

'You're crazy if you think I'll fall for that screwy invitation,' he breathed. 'Like hell you have Lita anywhere near the carny ground! But you've got her someplace. Let me tell you, Berg, if you harm her in any way I'll come gunnin' for you if I have to hell after you through every goddam State! I'll kill you, Berg, if you harm her! I'll — '

'Shaddup!' the brutish voice blazed. 'You're so smart — okay, get along to the carny ground at eight. Ya got a chance, bud. Ya gotta chance to locate the dame. What more d'ya want?'

And then the phone became a dead thing and Jerry moved it from his ear and stared at it stupidly. It was just reaction, and he cradled the instrument.

He knew damned fine just exactly what Tommy Berg's invitation meant. The guy just hated him and the invite was just bait to get his man where he would be easy prey for a fast slug or a bat on the head,

Nothing more than that. It was not a lead to the girl. It was just an invite to a death party because Tommy Berg wasn't satisfied in having grabbed the girl and the dope — he wanted to smash the private richard, too!

Jerry walked around his office and then flung down his hat. He lit a cigarette and just about consumed it in the first drag. He thought grimly there was time for a smoke. Sure he could tear up to the carny ground right away. Would it get him anywhere? He didn't know. He didn't know anything except that he was going to kill that louse, Tommy Berg, as soon as he got the chance. It was a pretty sombre decision because he was not a low hood with scant regard for human life, but a private detective with a licence to uphold the law.

He thought about the carny ground. He remembered passing the dump in his car a few times. A cheap ground where noisy rides and sideshows took fast dimes and nickels from punks, teenagers and young crooks. Right now it would be dead. As Tommy Berg had said, the ground started up at seven. And a guy wanted him to walk into the noisy place about eight. Why? Because it was dark then? Nope, couldn't be that because the ground was bright with electric light. Maybe it was because the place could become a noisy stage for sudden death via a fast slug!

Jerry Randell went to his window and stared down into Slausen. Sure, he'd go to the carny ground. It was a chance to tangle with Tommy Berg, the louse. He didn't expect Lita Rossini would be found at the carny place.

He'd go knowing he was walking into something that was nicely set up for his death. He couldn't do anything else but go.

The police? He did not think the cops could help unless they grabbed the three crooks unexpectedly. Just to slick the cops onto the carny ground would neutralise the whole thing.

Logically, there was nothing he could do until darkness sank over the cement jungle of Los Angeles and the neons flushed their greens, reds and yellows into the long straight streets. But he felt mighty restless. He couldn't sit in a damn office! He had to go out. Should he eat? He was probably too restless for even that.

He grabbed his hat again and went down to the street and got into his car. He figured he would drive over to Big Tom's Carnival and look the joint over with a new eye. Maybe he'd get an idea as to how to deal with the later rendezvous. He tooled away from the curb and joined the slow traffic stream. He drove down Slausen. A minute later he passed Hyde Park — that little bit of open space and greenery that bore the name of its counterpart in London, England. Fat, slug-shaped yellow cabs passed him, the drivers apparently tooling on their ulcers, to judge by their cutting tactics. The afternoon sun had spent its heat. The tall palms lining some of the streets still afforded shade to the indolent who parked on the seats beneath them.

Jerry Randell was driving slowly when he spotted one such guy. The man occupied most of the wooden bench. His bearded face identified him pretty fast.

Hairyface, the lunkhead!

Jerry tooled the car up to the kerb and pressed the horn. The short blast aroused the guy. He jerked and stared.

'Hiya, feller!' snapped Jerry Randell. 'You like a bench better than my office? Howsabout that wound? You ought to have it dressed.'

He might have known! All he got out of the man was a twisted grin and: 'Yak. Gurk. Wug. Ugh!'

Jerry said: 'All right, all right! I should have known. Get in this car an' I'll take you to a doc an' get that wound dressed.'

Hairyface shook his head firmly.

'Okay. You got any sense? Come along with me and we'll go to a drugstore. I'll buy bandages and lint and dress the damned thing for you. C'mon, get in — I ain't got all the time in the world if you have.'

This idea apparently appealed to Hairyface for he got up and opened the car door. Jerry felt sourly that the guy ought to take it easy with the door handle; he had nearly opened the door by wrenching the handle off! The man got in and sat beside him. Jerry drove off and wondered why the devil he was bothering with the lunkhead.

'You got any dough?' he snapped and then, looking at the man's tattered shirt and trousers, he asked: 'You had anything to eat?'

The question evidently touched off a subject that Hairyface understood for he solemnly patted his belly and pointed to his mouth and gave out with some hand signs in the dumb alphabet.

'You're hungry,' commented Jerry. 'And you got no dough. I'm hungry too, brother, but I got worries — that's the difference between you an' me, I guess, I got a sweet girl to worry about. You've got more sense than to get involved with a girl.' Jerry abruptly paused, remembering the time in the woods when Hairyface had carried Lita Rossini off. For a moment Jerry felt intense fury and then it subsided and he was grim, bitter. He remembered that Lita had pleaded with him to forget it.

Hairyface continued to make his hand

signs and Jerry Randell grinned faintly.

'Okay, I'll buy you some eats an' have that wound dressed. Don't know why the hell I'm doing it. Must be getting soft. I ought to kill you instead. I ought to have left you in that damned lake. Maybe I should take you to the cops. They'd give you a job sweeping up in the local pen.'

Instead of carrying out this programme, Jerry Randell stopped his auto at a drugstore and actually dressed the man's wound. It was, he discovered, a purely flesh wound and the slug had passed through and out. Even so, the wound would have hurt any other man. But not Hairyface, apparently. After leaving the drugstore and the curious proprietor, Jerry and the lunkhead went along to the nearest eats. The joint wasn't too classy, for which Jerry was duly thankful. They started into a solid spread which included eggs and ham, but apparently it wasn't solid enough for Hairyface because he made signs that most definitely indicated he wanted more.

Jerry got impatient even though the lunkhead ate fast enough. Eventually they left the diner and returned to the auto.

'You might as well know something.' muttered Jerry Randell as they sat back against the leather. 'Lita has been snatched by Tommy Berg — you know, the guy who hashed you around in order to get the dope. The guy had the gall to call me on the phone and invite me to Big Tom's Carnival ground tonight at eight. Just an invite to get killed. But he says I might find Lita Rossini that way. It's just a lead-on so he can smash me. The trouble is he knows I'll be there.'

Jerry Randell drove slowly as he talked and he managed to give Hairyface a comprehensive account of the position. He hardly knew why he talked to the man, but it seemed a slight relief to go over the facts.

Almost automatically, he had driven in the direction of Venice Boulevard. He was silent as he drove three miles down the wide street, passing the white, flat-roofed buildings, the hotels and stores. Then, all at once, he was level with the entrance to Big Tom's Carnival.

A gilded wooden entrance arch decorated the front of the carny ground. The place was dead. No sounds arose. The session did not start until later. Few folks were near the place, and Jerry could see only an odd guy in the ground itself — probably a carny man doing some work. A dead neon curved over the entrance arch and announced: *Big Tom's Carnival. Big Rides. Fun and Games.* At night it would be a pickup paradise for any punk with a big mouth and some dough. This was the sort of dive where teenage girls went wrong for the first time.

'Let's go in and take a looksee around the dump where I'm to be liquidated,' mocked Jerry Randell, and he tapped Hairyface on the arm.

They got out of the auto and walked into the carny ground. The big rides were silent and deserted. The sideshows were just quiet areas of flapping canvas. Two guys were laying a new cable in the cinder ground. They shot an odd glance at Jerry and his companion but that was all.

The private richard walked all around

the dump and noted the Tunnel of Love, the Rocket To Mars and a wicked-looking Somersaulter. It was just another carny ground. He cut through an alley and stared at the big trailers parked behind the sideshows. It was a commonplace and seemingly innocent scene, and it didn't look like Lita Rossini was hidden away in one of the trailers. Nope. It was all a damned gimmick to get him in the right sort of spot for a bump-off. Right now the scene was dead. At eight that night it could be transformed, a setting for a lousy design.

Jerry Randell tapped Hairyface's arm again. 'You get the idea — I'm to be bumped off in this place tonight at eight — or thereabouts. I guess that's it. A heater won't make much row against the noise of this dump goin' full blast. A pretty obvious setup!'

Maybe the lunkhead had no brains. But he nodded like a Hollywood yes-man. It seemed he understood.

Jerry turned sourly. 'Let's go back to the car!'

They tramped back. When they reached

the car Hairyface made some odd gestures and even grinned.

'You got a private life to lead, huh?' muttered Jerry. 'Okay. Beat it. I got enough grief without thinkin' how the hell you'll live.'

Jerry got into his car and lit a cigarette. He felt reluctant to leave the spot. What if Lita really was hidden away in one of those trailers? — but it was an incredible notion. These carny men were hardly likely to risk their good business for the sake of helping three thugs hide a snatched girl. Cheap and nasty though the carny ground might be, it was probably run on hard business lines and Big Tom was probably a guy with plenty to lose if he ran against the law.

Jerry smoked his cigarette and thought this rumpus had started as a business proposition. He'd been a guy ready to make an honest buck by tracking down the cached dope for the nutty Mr. Roedeck. Now it was something hellishly personal. Abe Craster's dope had lost its importance as an object for investigation. Instead, there was this brutish desire to

kill a guy — tear his goddam guts out
— over a girl!

He stubbed the cigarette butt in the dash ashtray. He decided it was no damned use sticking around. He'd be back at eight that night.

He'd be back to chance his luck against anything Tommy Berg would put over and the hell with him!

13

He spent his time sitting in the barroom drinking rye. He wasn't usually someone who drank such a lot but this night was different. He had gone past his usual amount and he was still cold sober. His head was an icy-cool globe where sombre, savage thoughts played in grim order. He sat in the barroom opposite his office on Slausen. Now and then he had gone over, unlocked and phoned the cop station in the hope there might be news. He did not underrate the cops. They had one smart organisation for locating wanted men and could achieve more than any lone private Richard could ever hope to do. But they had not found Tommy Berg, Cal Owen and Rick Egler. They had no trace of the missing girl and the dope had vanished.

Jerry lifted his glass and thought maybe that made the cops a lot of bums — but that wasn't right. The thugs were just having their run, that was all.

It was getting near to eight and his car was at the kerb. The neons battled triumphantly with the night air and the streets were full of autos and the sidewalks full of folks setting off to carve out their chunk of amusement for the night. And he sat and looked at his watch every two minutes.

Finally, Jerry Randell rose and walked out of the barroom, an ominous hunch to his shoulders.

He had his heater in his shoulder rig, and he also wore a neat stiletto in a calf-leather sheath strapped to his right leg.

He went to his car and drove away slickly, expertly. As to the rye he had consumed, he guessed it must have been water. Because it hadn't done anything to him.

He was really hating Tommy Berg now. The feeling lay heavily in his guts. He thought the rye had only fed the hate. It hadn't touched his brain.

He hated to even think for one moment that Lita had been in the hands of Tommy Berg a few hours now. He hated to think what might have happened to her. That was the sour, lousy part of it — the fact that he had been unable to help the girl.

He reached the carny ground and parked his auto the other side of the road where a chunk of waste land held a few other cars. He got out and walked steadily to the archway. The place was utterly different to the dead appearance it had presented only a few hours earlier. The neons blazed over the ornamental arch and announced in crimson that this was: *Big Tom's Carnival. Big Rides. Fun and Games.*

Yes, there would be fun and games!

He walked under the entrance arch and the red glare flushed down on to his set face; his jaw was craggy; his lips were a thin line. His shoes crunched on to the cinder-strewn ground and then the row really assailed him. The amplifiers hurled canned jazz tunes at him with a thunderous vibration that made his ears tingle. He slowed at once as he realised a gunshot would sound like a snapping shoelace in this dump!

184

Then he walked on again and his cheek gleamed as glaring electric light from a nearby shooting-gallery fell on it. He stopped, his back to a blank chunk of wood, and stared warily around. Just the usual crowd of punks and third-rate guys in cheap clothes moved around. Some giggling kids in sexy bargain basement dresses passed him, arm-in-arm, and they handed him a come-hither glance. There was some reason for it; at least he looked like a man in the crowd of punks! Even in his old duds.

He walked on again and licked dry lips. His eyes never ceased darting all over every inch of the way. He was looking for the slightest sign of anything unusual. He wasn't just looking for a man — he didn't think Tommy Berg would step out somewhere and take his hand!

He stopped again beside a whirling merry-go-round that was quite a vintage specimen. Some of the punks and girls were whirling around on crazy-looking wooden horses. The wild-looking mounts bobbed up and down in regular move-ment to the accompaniment of a savage blare of 'music'. The horses had ferocious, snorting heads and plunging hooves — or was it just imagination? Jerry Randell wondered and licked dry lips.

And then, as he stood looking at the crazy roundabout, he felt a sharp, angry whistle near his right ear. It was like the buzz of a jet-propelled wasp and the sound was only momentary. But he knew instantly what it was.

The shooting had started. The angry buzz had been a slug and it had missed. What was more he had not heard even the slightest sound of an exploding gun. He got it in a flash; not content with the row of the carny ground as a cover, the gunny was using a silenced gat!

All this in a flash of thought — and then Jerry Randell leaped for the gyrating wooden horses. He wanted to be moving fast, and this was obviously the quickest way! It was just an impulse, anyway. He was a man who worked on impulses, and this made him like a lot of other people!

As he jumped for the spinning platform, he was whirled back under the momentum. He hung on to a brass pole.

He quickly got the balance of the thing and he hauled himself up to the nearest riderless wooden horse.

He was in the saddle, so to speak, and he held the horse with one hand — his left, because his heater was bunched grimly in his right. As he whirled around he stared down at the flashing scene, at the few faces that stared up at the riders. There didn't seem anyone to connect with the solitary angry slug that had hissed past his ear. So the gunny had been in a hurry — the only way to account for the bad aim. Still another inch and the game would have come to an abrupt end. Jerry Randell, private richard, exit and candidate for a casket! But it had not been that way. Right now he was being whirled around on a bobbing wooden horse to the strains of a savage samba played on an amplifier with a decided rattle. He was looking for the would-be killer from this crazy vantage point.

Jerry went around about half a dozen times and then the carny guy made his way up to him on the gyrating machine.

The guy was indignant.

'Hey, ya jumped on the goddam thing — ya wanna break ya neck — ya ain't paid!'

Jerry turned his gun on the man, stared and hauled out a nickel from his trousers pocket. The carny guy flinched at the heater and took the coin and beat it. A moment later the roundabout slowed and finally came to a graceful halt.

Jerry got off fast and leaped to the cinder ground and bunched his gun in his jacket pocket, his fist around it. He'd shoot through the lining if necessary.

He almost ran to the nearest chunk of wood boarding that was part of a sideshow. He turned his back to it, pressed flat against the boarding and stared around grimly. At least his back was safe! He couldn't get a slug in the back. With keen grey eyes he stared again at the wandering crowds of punks and teenage girls. He thought he would spot the unknown gunny if he walked around openly because the man would look just that bit different somehow. And if Tommy Berg was doing his own gunning, he'd just need to lamp him once and there'd be hell to pay!

Jerry stood for fully a minute with his back to the boarding and thought so what was a minute against life or death. He deliberately calmed himself down. Maybe this was better played slow. Too fast a tempo and he might make a mistake. He was the hunted, at the moment, but he might turn the roles.

He turned his head and shot a scrutinising glance at the sideshow front only a yard away on his left. It was the first glance he had given it. Not that it really mattered. In his first look he saw it was a waxwork exhibition, a kind of old-fashioned racket that he figured would not appeal to the speed-crazy punks who patronised the carny ground.

Then Jerry Randell turned his head away — and a second later did a perfect double-take.

He stared back. Hard. He stared for one disbelieving second.

There was a guy standing at the entrance to the waxwork exhibition; the figure of a big man dressed in top hat and tails. The figure stood motionless, hands by its sides.

It could have been a wax dummy, and certainly looked like one. But in that first sharp glance Jerry Randell had seen something familiar about the dummy's face — and at the same time something mighty strange.

The motionless figure was a man he knew.

There was a carny guy at a pay box trying half-heartedly to get some of the drifting punks to enter the show. This guy moved. The tall figure in the shabby evening duds did not. It sure looked like a wax man. But it was not.

The figure was there to attract attention, but the gimmick wasn't working. Most of the punks who wandered past thought the figure was wax and left it at that.

Jerry knew it was a real guy, a big guy who had once worn a beard. The big guy had one affinity with a wax figure — he could not talk!

The guy was Hairyface, but he had had a shave. He looked very different, incredibly so. Jerry wet his dry lips and thought maybe his sharpened perceptions had enabled him to recognise the guy in his strange get-up and motionless stance.

It was bizarre, incredible. So the lunkhead had gotten himself a job on the carny ground, with a waxwork exhibition of all things! Jerry stole another glance at the strangely motionless man standing tall and oddly dignified in his top hat and tails. Yeah, Hairyface — only he couldn't be called that any more. It seemed he wasn't such a lunkhead either, but he'd have to bear that name!

Jerry moved. With his fist still bunched around his gun in his jacket pocket, he shuffled towards the pseudo wax figure. He wasn't forgetting the lurking killer but he figured he could pass the lunkhead and give him the wink.

Jerry stood in front of the wax show and looked up at the ornamental façade as if studying the announcements painted there. Lunkhead was just a yard away. Jerry lowered his glance and stared at the guy, a thin, knowing smile on his lips. He looked into the fixed stare of the motionless guy in top hat and tails.

Then the lunkhead's eyes glinted and the face twitched a bit. It was a swift signal to Jerry to look at the gloved hands.

Jerry shot a glance down. The hands cupped together low down, near the lower part of the guy's belly, and made swift signs in the dumb language. It was over in a second and then the hands were by the owner's side again and lunkhead was staring ahead once more. The signs had been brief and Jerry Randell's body had covered most of the movement.

But Jerry had got the message clear as a warning from hell. He thanked his lucky stars he knew enough about the dumb language of signs to decipher the message.

Tommy Berg was hiding in a shutdown sideshow less than fifteen yards away.

Jerry Randell stared up at the façade of the waxwork show again. He walked casually away, still giving the show the once-over like a guy who is idly curious. Then, anxious not to overdo the act, for Tommy Berg could be watching, he stared grimly around him and walked on with a little uncertainty.

So lunkhead had seen Tommy Berg on the carny ground. Maybe he had seen him snap off the first shot with the silenced gat. Anyway, lunkhead had seen plenty, enough to know that the gunny was lurking in the shutdown show on the other side of the alley. It seemed that lunkhead had more under his skull than one was ready to give credit. In fact, maybe he had got the job at the waxwork show just for the purpose of helping Jerry Randell. It was a great gimmick. The man could stand there and observe without anyone really noticing him. And without his beard and in his evening kit he looked completely different.

Jerry cut the ruminations. He'd get the facts out of lunkhead later — if he lived to see the man again.

He reached a big pillar that supported a big ride and halted, again with his back to the safety of solid wood. He stared sombrely down the alley towards the shutdown sideshow. Yeah, he ought to have guessed it was the ideal hideout for a lousy gunny.

Jerry stared, noting the salient features of the shutdown dump. Then he slowly turned his head. It wouldn't pay to give away the fact that he was interested in the shutdown joint. Tommy Berg might be watching him at this very moment — probably he was, wondering and waiting for the second when Jerry would walk again into the gunsight of his silenced gat.

The play had changed. Now that he knew where to locate Tommy Berg, they were both hunters.

Jerry stood for what seemed a long time but it was really only about five minutes. Out of narrowed eyes he shot a few glances at the dark patch of the shutdown sideshow, and then he finally figured out his intentions.

It was simple. It was stupidly simple. He was sick of the hell-around and there was only one real way to beat a guy who wanted to kill you — and that was kill the swine first. The hell with it! He'd walk down to the shutdown sideshow, like a guy who is just walking without any real destination. He'd walk like a guy who has every intention of passing the closed-up show. He'd be inviting a slug, but he figured it wouldn't come until he was right on the darkened dump.

But before he was really level with the shutdown place he'd move, but fast!

Above his head the noisy ride tore around at terrific speed and the row of canned music blared above the screams of the passengers. It was a grotesque background for the start of a walk that would lead to death — for someone!

He started. He moved slowly down the alley, like a guy who is returning along the same route after a fruitless walk. His head was sunk a little on his chin and his fist bunched around the heater in his jacket — but his finger was curled ready to trigger. He went on, the yards steadily diminishing between him and the dark ominous hole that was the hideout of the gunny.

He didn't doubt that Tommy Berg was still there. He had not left from the moment lunkhead had given him the tip because Jerry had really never taken his eyes off the joint. Yeah, the swine was there, lurking like some obscene beast. He stood for all sorts of lousy, rotten things . . . Lita in some hideaway . . . man-handled by some louse . . . dirt, danger and death . . . and beyond that the dope distribution which would push some suckers even further down the path of wretchedness. Tommy Berg stood for all that. But right now the issue was simple. Who was to die?

Jerry walked on. He saw the brightly illuminated facade of the wax show and lunkhead standing motionless in his upper-crust duds. Just across the same alley was the dark place where the killer lurked. The whole thing was kind of horrible.

And then there were only three more yards to go and he'd be level with the shutdown dump.

And when he was level a slug would hiss out and spell the end of the line for Jerry Randell.

Like hell!

He leaped like some enraged beast with murder in its heart. Sheer animal fury gave him tremendous fury, gave him tremendous impetus. He just travelled the three yards like someone shot out of a gun. He had to get hellish speed or meet a slug coming out of that ominous dark hole.

He got it. He was busting into the dark place via a small arch that served as a door. He plunged into the hole and with sickening anger realised the gloom wasn't to his advantage. He did not slacken his furious charge for a second. Immediately he found himself inside the place, he fell to the floor, scampered along like an animal.

A gun flashed at once from a corner of the gaunt structure and a slug bit into wood behind Jerry Randell. There was no explosion; just a dull plop.

The orange flash gave the gunny's position away. Jerry hardly stopped his frantic scrambling. He slid across the grimy cement floor like some ugly reptile going after its prey. He didn't shoot. He wanted Tommy Berg dead but he didn't want the slob to die fast.

A guy can talk before he dies.

Another flash of the silenced gat licked

out just as Jerry grabbed at the man's feet and once again the slug was just a vicious bit of metal cutting thin air. The darkness wasn't helping Tommy Berg now. He wasn't a guy in the dark taking careful shots at another guy out in a brilliantly-lit carny ground.

Within a second the whole thing changed as Jerry Randell tugged Berg off his balance. The man crashed down and turned into a savage, fighting for his very life. Jerry knew from the start he was going to beat this lug. He was going to beat hell out of him because killing the man was nothing if he didn't get Lita safe. He smacked his gun butt into the man's face. Then he smashed clawing hands to one side and planted a vicious punch that nearly went through Tommy Berg's gullet and into the cement.

It seemed that Berg had lost his silenced gat in his fall.

Jerry grinned in the darkness and slid his hands around the man's throat. He started the long squeeze that usually ends in death. Strangling isn't a nice business. Tommy Berg quit milling fists and grabbed frantically at Jerry's wrists and shook them, rammed and tugged at them. But it wasn't any use. Jerry had cut off the man's breath and hell was leering at him.

Tommy Berg writhed his body and Jerry felt it was rotten sitting astride a dying carcass. The man clawed deep grooves in Jerry's rock-like wrists. Blood ran promptly. It came warm and sticky inside Jerry's strangler hands but he didn't mind or even feel the pain caused by the other's frantic gouging.

And then, when he knew that Tommy Berg was dying, he slackened the revolting pressure. He eased his hands away and heard the slob gulp for life-saving air. So he wasn't dead yet!

'You know where Lita is! Give! Where is she? Start talkin' and I'll let you live.' Jerry shook the man in a fury of impatience. 'Talk, blast you!'

Because Tommy Berg knew the horror of approaching death, he gasped into hoarse words. His throat was just about crushed but he managed to hack out sounds that made sense.

'She's with . . . others . . . at Joe Spesler's . . . aauugh . . . '

Berg's voice choked off into wet, slobbery sounds. Jerry shook him again. 'C'mon, talk. You mean Spesler, the dope racketeer? At his hideout? Where's that? C'mon, talk an' you live!'

Again a spasm of desperate speech coming from a practically mutilated throat. 'Spesler . . . dive . . . on 4th Street . . . beneath the Frolic . . . night . . . '

Jerry flung the man to one side. The information was his and he didn't doubt it was the truth. A man in Tommy Berg's position has a lot to gain by talking true.

'Okay — you live! I said you would. I ought to kill you. I don't know why the hell I don't! But I don't want to wake up at nights screaming. I don't want leprous hands!'

Jerry got up; took a yard towards the purple of the sideshow entrance.

At that moment a big figure in good-fitting clothes pushed into the gaunt show structure and took two large strides to the sprawling man. Jerry knew the figure was lunkhead in his top hat and tails. He knew, too, the big dumb guy was hell-bent to grab Tommy Berg. For good reasons; because Tommy Berg had chopped him around and thrown him in a lake to drown.

Jerry reacted too late. There were aches in his body as the result of the tension of the past few minutes and it slowed him — the inevitable reaction that will slow any human being.

Lunkhead grabbed Tommy Berg and in the same vicious movement slammed the man's head down on the concrete floor. Jerry was turning back as lunkhead raised the senseless man and banged his head down horribly once more. There was a sickening thud. Jerry pulled lunkhead away but received a powerful push that sent him back. As he came at the big dumb brute again, lunkhead rammed Tommy Berg's head to the ground for the third and last time.

Jerry turned and staggered out of the dark enclosure. He walked fast but unsteadily through the blare and glare of the carny ground. Everything seemed to bawl at him — successive wafts of crazy music. He stared unseeingly at the tearing rides and the blinking lights.

Then he was through the entrance arch and he felt calmer and steadier and he thought the night air was cooler, but that was just imagination, of course!

He got to his car and piled in. He lit a cigarette, stared at the distant carny ground, realised he'd beaten the in-bitten Tommy Berg. Only now did it seem real.

He drove away fast, leaving the dead man, the carny ground, lunkhead in his grotesque top hat and tails. He didn't want to ever damn-well see them again.

His first call was the cop station, and he sang such a song that cop cars were immediately crewed and driven out of the station garage with whining sirens and blinking roof-top indicator lights,

They raced with slick, unbelievable speed through the neon-lit chasms that were the L.A. streets and slid to a halt beside the Frolic Nite Spot on 4th Street.

Jerry Randell went in with the gang of cops and even the Captain couldn't stop him.

All because of a sweet girl with red hair

and greenish, defiant eyes!

Well, history has been made on less and this was just another night in the cement jungle for the Los Angeles Police Department.

* * *

Jerry Randell, private richard with an easy mind, walked upstairs with his hand round the soft, pliant waist of Lisa Rossini. They went upstairs to his office,

'You've got everythin',' he said in wonderment. 'You're some girl. The grief has just slid off you like the troubles of a kid's life.'

'Look, let's forget, huh?' She turned her head and rolled her red lips softly against his face. 'Just say I'm mighty glad that run-around is over. I never want to be hauled out of Spesler's dive again — even by a cute guy like you.'

'Okay, we forget,' he agreed. 'An' let's talk about something different. That damned dope is rounded up and those two traffickers, Cal Owen and Rick Egler, will get a nifty stretch. Me — I get my account settled by Mr. Roedeck.' He kissed her again.

'You got something on your mind?' she mocked.

'In my mind, in my hair, under my skin!'

'Gee, will it always be like this?'

'Should be. How the devil should I know?'

'Will you marry me? Guess you'll have to — if what I think is on your mind is right!'

'Yeah, why not?'

They went on up the stairs together.

THE END

We do hope that you have enjoyed reading this large print book.

Did you know that all of our titles are available for purchase?

We publish a wide range of high quality large print books including:
Romances, Mysteries, Classics
General Fiction
Non Fiction and Westerns

Special interest titles available in large print are:
The Little Oxford Dictionary
Music Book, Song Book
Hymn Book, Service Book

Also available from us courtesy of Oxford University Press:
Young Readers' Dictionary
(large print edition)
Young Readers' Thesaurus
(large print edition)

For further information or a free brochure, please contact us at:
Ulverscroft Large Print Books Ltd.,
The Green, Bradgate Road, Anstey,
Leicester, LE7 7FU, England.
Tel: (00 44) 0116 236 4325
Fax: (00 44) 0116 234 0205

Other titles in the
Linford Mystery Library:

CALL IN THE FEDS!

Gordon Landsborough

In Freshwater, Captain Lanny was an honest cop with problems: his men and his chief were on the take from the local gangster Boss Myrtle. Bonnie, Myrtle's daughter, was in love with Lanny, but he couldn't pursue the relationship because of her father's criminal activities. Lanny's problems multiplied as Freshwater became threatened by an influx of murderous criminals from New York — a gang of bank raiders, and Pretty Boy, a psychotic murderer of young women. Then Bonnie went missing . . .

THE EDEN MYSTERY

Sydney J. Bounds

Interstellar entrepreneurs, the Eden clan, had opened up new planets, building a galactic empire, governed by the United Worlds' Federation. However, stability is threatened by an impending war between the worlds of Technos and Mogul. The Federation fears intervention by the clan's sole survivor, Kyle Eden. Meanwhile, Hew Keston is investigating the Eden family's history for the media corporation Stereoscopic Inc. But his life is in danger — someone is stopping him from learning the secrets of the Eden clan!

THE LOST FILES OF SHERLOCK HOLMES

Paul D. Gilbert

Dr John Watson finally reopens the lid of his old tin dispatch box and unearths a veritable treasure trove of unpublished tales recounting the remarkable skills of his friend and colleague, Mr Sherlock Holmes. With the detective's consent, we are now finally privileged to witness how Holmes, with his customary brilliance, unravelled the secrets lurking within a too-perfect police constable, a Colonel with a passion for Arthurian mythology, and the public house which never sold a single pint of ale . . .

SCARE TACTICS

David Whitehead

These seven short stories take you on a trip through the twilight world of the supernatural, which include: the terrifying universe where men fall in love with monsters; a troubled child's nightmares which prove to be real; a house which attracts evil much as a sponge attracts water; and demons, from a time before history, making Satanic pacts in order to return from the past. Not a journey for the faint-hearted — there will be no shortage of scare tactics.

F.B.I. SPECIAL AGENT

Gordon Landsborough

Cheyenne Charlie, Native American law student turned G-Man, is one of the Bureau's top agents. The New York office sends for him to investigate a sinister criminal gang called the Blond Boys. Their getaway cars somehow disappear in well-lit streets; they jam police radios; and now they've begun to add brutal murder to their daring robberies. Cheyenne follows a tangled trail that leads him to a desperate fight to the death in the beautiful scenery of the Catskill Mountains . . .